Vicky,
Thank you for your support!
Happy reading! I hope it
love with the t:
Ho Ho Ho! M

Secret Santa

Keren Hughes

ISBN 978-1-912768-24-0

Published 2018
Published by Black Velvet Seductions Publishing

Secret Santa Copyright 2018 Keren Hughes
Cover design Copyright 2018 Jessica Greeley

Acknowledgments

Where, oh where to start... I hate writing acknowledgments in a way. I always feel like I'm going to miss somebody out and they'll be offended. So, I'm going to preface this by saying; if I don't mention you by name, please don't be offended. I'm still grateful and I still love you, I just take too much morphine and have a short memory span. (One reason I hate being disabled.)

So, who to thank first...? I also don't want to offend people by not putting them first. But honestly, the person I need to thank most for this book read it before anyone else. She helped me shape the characters and the story. She's only 17 years old, but she has the maturity of a 30-year-old and she is a great sounding board, she loves my ideas, she sees them all play out in her head and gets all excited. When I told her I was writing a Christmas story, she was so excited. She kept screaming for more as I wrote it. I wrote faster so that I could give her something. Every single time, her comments were bang on the money. She couldn't stop praising this book and heralding it as the best book I've written so far. It amazes me how much love and support she shows me. Jodie Harrold, I want to say that thank you is not enough. I cannot fathom the love and admiration that flows from you to me. You always tell me you're so proud of me and it makes my smile beam from ear to ear. It sends the warm and fuzzies all the way to my black heart! I love you, lady. You amaze me. I hope you'll always read my books and enjoy them as much as you did Secret Santa. Thank you for loving Preston and Nye almost as much as I do. It means the world to know you support me and have faith in me, even when I don't. If I don't tell you this enough, I love you!

Kara Stewart, they should make an award for world's best PA. You wouldn't win, but they should make an award for that. Just saying! No, seriously, you are the best PA I could have ever wished for. Your enthusiasm for everything I write, even when you are poorly, you still beg me for more. I'd say in the pecking order, I write mostly for myself, but then I write for you, Jodie, Chele and Trudy, then everybody else. You're my tribe and I LOVE you all. But you, well, you are my "Scrote-sack." There you go, I used it in a book after all! Thank you for all the moral support you give me. There may be a big pond separating us, but I can feel the love you give all the way over here. Your enthusiasm knows no bounds and you are always excited for me to write new characters and their stories. I thank Justine for introducing us. I don't know where I'd be without you. Thank you for being my biggest cheerleader. All you need now is pom-poms.

Chele McKenzie, where to start… well…I love you. You are amazing. You pick me up when I am down, you make me smile even when I want to frown. You keep the dream alive in me. Your love and support mean so much to me that mere words cannot express it. I'm so glad we met. I wouldn't be where I am now if it wasn't for you. Sometimes, I want to quit writing and you always list the reasons why I shouldn't give it all up. You're too good for me. You're my bestie. I love you from the top of your head to the tip of your toes. You're part of my tribe and I know you'll never leave me. A friendship like ours is special. Friendship is a two-way street—some people forget that—and you just show me that I was right when I thought you could be the kindest person I've ever had the pleasure of knowing. You amaze me. Your enthusiasm for my stories, your help in proof-reading, your love of my characters; you're invaluable to me. Always.

Trudy Moore, you're my slapper and I love you. You always text me things like "Oh my god, I can't believe you left me hanging" or "Oh my god, I need more, NOW" and those texts always make me smile. You're so enthusiastic about my characters and their stories. I love that you are my sounding board. Just like the other girls in my tribe, I can always count on you for guidance, moral support and boundless love. You pick me up, dust me off and make me try again when I believe I am failing at this job. You amaze me, and I love you more every day. Thank you isn't enough, but seriously; THANK YOU.

Nan, I love you more than words could ever say. You're not my nan, you're my mom and you taught me how to be me. Thank you for everything you have ever done for me in the last 35 years. Honestly, I don't know how you put up with me. Thank you for always buying my books and supporting me. I LOVE YOU.

Calum, my darling son, what can I say about you? You're not old enough to read my books—and you'll never be old enough in my eyes. Thank you for being my rock, my anchor in the storm, my sunshine on rainy days. Thank you for bringing a love to my life that I had never known before giving birth to you. You're the best thing in my life and I am so freaking proud of you. You always tell everyone "my mom is an author" and though that makes me blush profusely, I'm glad you're proud of me. You are what makes my heart beat. You are my world and everything in it. Thank you for the last 11 years. I can't wait to spend the rest of my life watching you grow into the amazing young man I know you will be because you are already halfway there. I love you, kiddo.

Richard Savage, you're the best boss in the universe. You love my stories, you love my characters, you love my writing. That means the world to me! I cannot thank you enough for repeatedly taking a chance on me and publishing my words. Thank you for being a wonderful man that I trust, respect and look up to.

Jessica Greeley, Thank you for yet another amazing cover design. And for also rocking my socks with matching bookmarks. You rock!

My wonderful tribe, you all know who you are. Karen Rock—aka Wonder Woman—you're always so proud of me and your support means more than I can say. Justine McFadyen, thank you for being my friend, my cheerleader, my rock. Susan Scott, thank you for being crazy about my stories and for the beautiful reviews you write. Your words mean more to me than mine do to you, trust me on that! Lisa Morgan, thank you for being such a great friend. You are always super-supportive and kind, generous and sweet. Friends like you are hard to come by. Claire Jenni Alexander, thank you for being you. You just get me. Like, really get me. On another level to most people. Thank you for being the kindest, most amazing friend who loves me for me and doesn't want to change me. I love you.

To my readers, thank you for taking a chance on me. Thank you for everything, your reviews, your support, EVERYthing.

To the people who leave good reviews, thank you for each and every amazing word you have said about me. It means the world to me. I am where I am because of my readers and you all help new readers find out about me with your reviews. So, thank you from the bottom of my heart.

To the people who leave me bad reviews, thank you. I read those reviews and take what I need to become a better writer.

To the amazing bloggers, you all help me so much and I am honored and humbled by your support. I am crazy about you all. So, thank you for everything you do. I am truly blessed.

To my new group, Sass & Snark ARC Group, thank you for being a part of my life, a part of my crew and a part of each new book I write. I hope you enjoy all the ARCs I'm going to shower you with. I couldn't do it without you guys!

To each and every person reading this book and any of my others, thank you for taking a chance on me. You freaking rock!

To readers old and new…this one is for you! I hope you enjoy it.

Prologue

Once upon a time, here in the small town of Snowflake, everything was as close to perfect as you could get. The town thrived, stores always did good trade and the people always smiled like their hearts were full to bursting. We chatted, we laughed, we all got along. That was until the new mayor came along. She wanted to introduce—what she called "better"—business strategies. She brought with her a shit-ton of pie charts, graphs, all sorts of things that someone with a background in business, someone with a degree in it, would bring with them. The new mayor sucked. Literally. She drained the life out of our small town. Instead of attracting business, she pushed it away…in droves.

Soon the once thriving businesses were going bust. What had gone wrong? The mayor couldn't answer that. But I could. She'd come in on her high horse with her grand plans to renovate an already thriving town and she'd decimated just about everything instead. How? That I'm not sure about. Maybe she made the business owners unhappy. Maybe she thought that there was room for improvement—even though nobody else in town felt that way. Maybe she backed people into a corner and, rather than suffer under her, they decided to move away, taking their business to where it could continue to do well, out of her reach.

I'm not saying that some of her ideas weren't good. I'm not saying that everything she suggested was wrong. But when Snowflake started looking like a ghost town, that's when she finally gave up trying, decided to resign as mayor and hightailed it out of town, back the way she'd come. Only this time, she wasn't on a high horse. She no longer lived in an ivory tower, ordering people to "do as she said". This time, she knew that not even her business degree was going to save her.

What could our small town do to attract business owners back? What could we do to bring people back to line our streets with smiles on their faces? It seemed that very little could be done, and we were going to fade into insignificance while our neighboring towns continued to enjoy the boost to their economy.

The day Preston Wolfric Fitzgerald III arrived in Snowflake was a day we'd never forget. He came promising he'd undo all the bad that the previous mayor had done. He swore he'd help heal our town. Trouble was, his heart wasn't really in it. He'd been sent by his grandfather, Preston Wolfric Fitzgerald I, a man who made his fortune off the misery of others. He strode around like he was untouchable—his ice-cold manner doing nothing to endear him to people—and he razed everything to the ground so he could continue to build his empire. I never met the guy and I can't say I was sorry when I heard he'd passed away. His son had died at the tender age of forty-three, a heart attack by all accounts. So, his grandson had inherited the company and everything that went with it. That's when he came to Snowflake and started to help us rebuild.

Preston Wolfric Fitzgerald III was just as untouchable as you would think a man with a name like that would be. He was rich, filthy rich, and outrageously handsome—so handsome it should be a crime, for which he'd end up in jail for a life sentence—his dark hair and dark, brooding eyes made him painful to look at. His chiseled jaw and slick-backed hair made him look like a model straight off the cover of GQ magazine. Of course, his looks were the only good thing about him. Other than that, he had no admirable traits. He was stuffy, flash, stubborn and bordered on being an arrogant ass. Did I say bordered on? I mean he *was* an arrogant ass.

Seriously, I don't know where it is that they breed men like him, but wherever it is, they need to start thinking of installing more endearing qualities in their handsome, infuriating jerk excuses for men. And if this is what the men are like, heaven forbid I meet a woman made of the same stock. I'd probably end up in jail for doing something I would later realize I didn't regret.

To this day, Preston Wolfric Fitzgerald III makes me mad as hell. I'll give him his due—although it took him a while, he did actually attract business back to our town. He did bring our little town into the twenty-first century—which is actually an improvement on how it was before, just don't tell him I said that. But he's also infuriating and smug, and drives a sleek black Bugatti Veyron, which I am totally jealous of.

He only wears Armani suits that must cost a bare minimum of

about three month's wages to me. I have to admit, a handsome man in a well-tailored suit is somewhat a turn on. A black three-piece suit, with a crisp white shirt and a black tie to complete the look, this man really is the epitome of … well, I can't quite describe it actually … he's … knee-quakingly desirable. Is that even a thing? If not, it should be. He made me melt into an incoherent puddle of goo at his feet the moment I met him. He shook my hand and I felt the electricity run up my arm and zip all the way down my spine. I'm one of the only three original businesses left in this town—well, not me, my store is, but you catch my drift. I stood there in front of this Adonis and my mouth went as dry as the Sahara. I felt like I'd been eating cotton wool or something because I couldn't produce saliva, never mind words.

His hand had dwarfed mine and it felt like mine was made to fit in his palm. His Patek Phillipe watch glinted in the sunlight and the hairs on his forearm were a stark contrast to mine. I don't know why I kept making so many mental comparisons between us, it's not like he was here to hook up with me—not that I like "hooking-up" with guys, I'm not built that way. I actually prefer real relationships to random sex. But this man made me quiver at the mere touch of his hand on mine. If that's what he could do when he wasn't trying, I'd hate to see what he could do when he really put his mind to it. Why, oh why, had I been thinking about what an orgasm from this man would feel like when all I actually wanted to do was smack him in his far too gorgeous face?!

Broad shoulders had caught my attention and I was mentally berating myself for getting distracted when he was talking about my business and its role here in Snowflake. I'd missed most of what he'd said and realized I was never going to admit that to him. He'd think I was a complete moron—if he didn't already—and I didn't want to give him any ammunition against me in case he decided to try and crush my business under his—no doubt designer—shoe while he brought someone in that he thought could do a better job.

I'll be a grown-up—I'm a mature, sensible woman, after all—and admit that Snowflake is now better than the once thriving town it used to be. And it's all thanks to Mr. Handsome. But his arrogance is his downfall. He's a little like the ex-mayor, thinking that, because he has money and business acumen, everyone will bow down to him and lick his—like I say, no doubt designer—shoes. But while everyone else in this town is either under his spell, or at least begrudgingly doing his bidding, I am bucking against his leadership—much like I wish I was bucking my hips as I grind myself against him—and I am going to keep doing things my way. My store did well for itself before he came along, and I am determined that it will stay that way long after he's got bored of fulfilling his grandfather's wishes and has left this town behind him in his Bugatti's rearview mirror.

I'm Nye Mackenzie—or as my mother calls me, Aneurin—and Snowflake is my home. It's where I was born and where I'll die. I am determined to show Mr Pearly-White Grin that Snowflake is more than a business empire. It's a home. Full of happy families who have been here for generations before he came along and will have descendants here long after he's left. It's somewhere I want to have a family of my own one day. Or I would if an ex-boyfriend didn't live around every corner.

I'm not a slut or anything, the town is just that small that a lot of people have dated each other here and I'm no different. But I don't want children with any of those exes; I don't want to marry the cocky, self-assured, self-obsessed asshole I was engaged to this time last year. Why had I ever wanted to become Mrs. Aneurin Dacre anyway? What kind of stupid name was that? I mean, come on, my mother already gave me a stupid first name—pronounced "an-eye-rin'—so why did I need a stupid surname to go with it? Dacre—pronounced "dayker" in case you were wondering—two stupidly pronounced names meshed together. Yeah, I was glad I'd given that a swerve.

Yes, there was a time when I'd once considered myself the luckiest girl in the world that Mal had looked at me like I was the only woman on Earth. But then I'd caught him playing around with some floozy waitress from the dive bar in the next town over. That was enough to put him on my shit list for life. Not that he didn't try to earn my love back with stupid romantic gestures and shit. But I wasn't interested then, and I'm not interested now. I'm happily single. Living my life and doing things my own way. My store is doing well and that's enough for me.

So, why is it that I catch myself wondering what life would be like if I was Mrs. Aneurin Fitzgerald?

I'm not a person who is impressed by money or flash cars or expensive things—I've never been the materialistic type—but sometimes I wonder if I could scale the walls of Preston's ivory tower and bring him down to reality. Why do women think they can change men? I could never catch a man like that's eye, let alone tame his heart.

No doubt he has women falling at his feet everywhere he goes. All he has to do is flutter those long eyelashes or give them the puppy-dog eyes and they'd shed their clothes and fall into his bed. No doubt he'd give them the best sex of their lives and then discard them like a used tissue. A man like him looks like he'd have impressive sexual prowess. He oozes sex appeal from every pore.

Look at me, talking like I'm bothered what he'd be like in bed—whether he could give me an orgasm to make my toes curl—or what he does with his life. It's none of my business and I really don't care. He can bed all the women in this town and I still wouldn't care.

I should really be focusing on my own life. On my store. On Christmas, which is just around the corner.

Christmas is a big occasion in Snowflake. The people in town seem to care that we have a name synonymous with the occasion, so they decorate like it's going out of fashion. We literally have the biggest tree in the town center. It gets decorated and then we have an official tree-lighting ceremony where all the residents and out-of-towners gather to watch it come to life.

We have a new mayor, one much less like her predecessor. She cares about the town and its people. She comes out to officially light our tree and join in the celebrations. Unlike Mr "Moneybags" who probably sits at home, brooding, without a tree and devoid of Christmas spirit—much like Ebenezer Scrooge—drinking expensive whiskey from a decanter, God forbid he pour it from the bottle.

In fact, he probably doesn't pour it at all. He probably has a manservant—or should I be saying *butler*—do all that for him. A maid to clean his far from humble home. A home that's probably so big he rattles about in it, occupying only a fraction of its space. He probably has a chauffeur to drive him into Snowflake. I wouldn't know, it's not like I actually watch when he arrives or departs. I might, if I knew when he was coming. But then again, maybe not. After all, I don't care for his comings and goings. At least that's what I tell myself. I do know one thing; this is his first Christmas in Snowflake and we are aiming to make it our best yet. Most people are probably out to impress him, kissing his oh-so-shiny shoes. Not me. I'm going to make this Christmas my best yet purely because it makes me feel good. I don't care what Mr "Flash with The Cash" thinks. Oh, who am I even kidding here? Myself, mostly.

Chapter One

Nye

"This Christmas display will be the death of me," my assistant, Paisley, remarks.

"More likely the boss will be the death of you if you don't help her get it right," I reply with a wink and a grin.

"Why did you have to volunteer our help to your bloody mother, Nye? Her ideas are always grandiose and goddamn awful to boot."

That's true. My mother has great taste and a great eye for interior design, but when it comes to Christmas, she is full-on. If you ask me, sometimes less is more. But if you ask my mother, she'll always say that it needs "more this" or "more that". She can't see that she needs to scale back her tacky Christmas decorations.

I shouldn't say they're tacky, they usually cost her a fortune. She doesn't buy "mass produced" stuff, it's usually bespoke, one of a kind. But just because something is a one-off with a hefty price tag, that doesn't mean it's necessarily pretty to look at. My mother has this thing for shiny little trinkets, saying she has an eye for pretty things, like a magpie. In reality, some of it looks like you could pick it up at a flea market. Not that I would ever tell Evelyn that. I just smile and nod. It's better to appease Evelyn Mackenzie than it is to try and go against her. I've gone toe-to-toe with her many times in my thirty-one years on this earth. And I've lost more battles than I can count on both of my hands and feet combined.

"You know Evelyn goes OTT. Every damn year she wants the biggest, the best, the most expensive."

"Yeah, I'm just glad it's not my store she's decorating."

The one and only year I had allowed her to help me design a display for my clothing boutique, she had made it look like some cheap, crass-looking—I don't actually have words for it, but believe me, it was farcical and awful. Paisley begged me to never let my mother take the reins again, and I had to completely agree. Once she'd left the store, we had to take a few things down and put them in the storeroom. I just couldn't stand to look at a place that looked like Dr. Seuss had thrown up Christmas on it.

"Holy crap!" Paisley exclaims as she nearly drops her end of the large ornament we are trying to squeeze into the badly thought-out display.

How can my mother have such an eye for normal, everyday interior design, but be so awful when it comes to Christmas? And how did she rope me into helping put it all together for her? When I say help, I mean do it for her. Hence why I'd asked Paisley to help, because Evelyn had other things she needed to attend to. Some function or other is of higher importance than silly little things like actually doing your own decorating. Yes, that's heavy on the sarcasm.

Evelyn Mackenzie has far more important things to do than anything that remotely resembles having to get her hands dirty. She used to be less standoffish and more like an actual mother, a real human being. However, since she divorced my father, men have been courting her attention. They're always trying to impress her with some fancy cordon bleu restaurant or something. Trouble is, we don't have many of those in town. We also don't have many single men over a certain age—fifty-four—in town, so she has to limit her expectations. They can't all have fat chequebooks and deep pockets.

At one point, my mother didn't either, it was when she and my father divorced three years ago that she got more money. Dad was the rich one. Sometimes I think she married him for love and other times, I wonder if it wasn't a little—if not a lot—to do with his bank balance. When they split up, I was happy. She seemed to drain my dad of any energy. She's enough to sap a power station, in all honesty. Not many kids say they're happy when their parent's divorce, but I wasn't a kid, I was twenty-eight, and I had seen firsthand what their marriage had been like.

I'm sure they loved each other when they first got together and when they first had me. But by the time they'd been married for thirty-three years, it had taken its toll on them both. Pretending can be so hard. This is why I want someone to love me for me and not what my bank balance looks like or what they stand to gain from being with me, other than my love and all that comes with it, of course.

"Thank f—I mean, thank goodness that's done," Paisley says as she stands back to survey the display.

"You don't say. And Evelyn isn't here, you can say fuck."

She giggles and looks at me. "I just feel like a naughty schoolgirl who's going to get her mouth washed out with soap for cursing."

"Trust me, me too when she's around. Always have to be on my guard for what comes out of my mouth. I actually have to think before I speak. She once did wash my mouth out with soap."

"She did not?" Paisley gasps, covering her mouth with her hand.

"I was about eighteen. I was drunk. She didn't like it. Nor did my dad, but he's not a jerk with a stick up his ass, unlike my mother. Don't worry, it was only a tiny bit of soap and my dad yanked it out of her hand like lightning. He didn't speak to her for the next couple of days, swearing straight up and down it was akin to some sort of child abuse."

"Thank god for Beckett."

"Yeah, I thought he'd have a bloody stroke or something, the way he ripped into her for doing it. I was upstairs in my room and I could hear them as clear as crystal."

"I always feel like I'm about twelve years old around Evelyn. She scares me."

"I feel like an errant child too, and I'm thirty-one. Sometimes I adore my mother, and other times, I think she should be grateful I'm still talking to her."

As if talking about the devil could make them appear, I hear my mother's key in the lock.

"Oh no, girls, that Santa is in completely the wrong place," she chides as she sees our display.

"Mother, we've followed your very detailed instructions. That's where you said he's supposed to be."

"Yes, well, now I see it in person, I want it moved. In fact…"

She goes on to make us move some of the decorations around. Not lifting a finger to help, Evelyn dictates while Paisley and I do all the hard work.

"It's nearly perfect, girls, it's just that I can't help but feel something is missing."

Missing? She has just about everything you could imagine here and yet she wants more? Typical Evelyn Mackenzie. Anal retentive is how best to describe her. What she wants, she gets. Typically, I am the one to furnish her every need.

"We've got to get back to the store, mother. I'm sorry. We have our own display to perfect before we open in the morning. I can't open while everything is strewn about everywhere."

"Oh yes, dear. You get along and do just that. Don't worry about me. I'll figure out what I'm missing and then you can come and sort it out for me."

Heaven forbid I embarrass my mother, which is why I invented the excuse to get out of here. If she thinks the store is a mess, she will think it reflects on her—because *everything* is about her—and she wouldn't want that.

At long last, Paisley and I can finally leave this godforsaken place and grab a bottle of wine and a takeaway. It's been a long-ass day. My limbs are weary from hefting heavy objects around for hours. Poor Paisley must be shattered. It's a good job she'd do anything for her best friend. She'd never have let me do all this on my own. She knows only too well what my mother is like.

Having grown up together, gone to school together, been there for all the milestones in each other's lives, I love Paisley like the sister I never had.

She was only too happy to come and work for me when I got *Style in Snowflake* up and running. I had the business acumen and the idea for the store and Paisley has the eye for design. She helps to choose the clothes we stock. She has a unique sense of style and it's worked well for the store over the years. She's so much more than just my assistant and I am grateful to have her in my life. So much so, that I want to offer her a share in the business—she just doesn't know it yet. I'm planning on it being her Christmas present.

"Thank you, mother. We'll get going and leave you to it," I say, grabbing Paisley's arm and pulling her along to make our great escape.

"Of course, darling. You need that store looking shipshape and Bristol fashion."

Such an odd turn of phrase, but that's my mother for you.

Paisley and I make good our escape and jump into my car—a Mercedes Benz E Class that my mother bought me for my thirtieth birthday. I'd always driven a little Honda Civic and I loved that car, but my mother wants me to keep up appearances. All that matters to her is how things look from the outside. I didn't want the new car, but I couldn't reject her gift, even though it was purchased with some of the money she got when she divorced my father. So, I drive this sleek black car around because it's what's expected of me and I bite my lip and refrain from saying something I might later regret.

"God I'm glad to be out of there," Paisley says as she searches my playlist.

"Santa Baby" by Eartha Kitt begins to play and Paisley sings along in that sweet voice of hers.

***

Full up from the takeaway, Paisley and I sit back with a glass of wine in hand. It's nice to just sit in my lounge and relax. My Christmas tree in the corner is decorated tastefully; garlands adorn the inglenook fireplace and windowsills. It looks homely and full of festive spirit in here. Very much unlike my mother, my taste is … minimalistic, I guess. Some might say sparse, but I think it's just enough.

My iPod is playing quietly in the background—Christmas songs, of course. It's nice to be able to sit here with my feet up, a blanket wrapped around me, made by my grandmother, with my best friend making idle chitchat.

We told my mother a white lie—or technically I told her the lie, not Paisley—because the store looks perfect. We got all our decorating done last night, knowing I had to take today off to help my mother. That was our last day off in the run-up to Christmas though, except for Sundays, when the store is always closed. Though in the couple of weeks before Christmas, I open up on Sundays too. I give Paisley the time off to spend as she chooses, knowing I can handle the odd day without her there.

This is the busiest time of the year, so enjoying a glass or two of wine is my way of relaxing my overworked muscles.

Paisley decides to go home and get an early night, knowing we have an early start tomorrow. After seeing her off in a cab, I turn off all the lights downstairs, including those on the tree, I make my way up to my room and strip off before walking into my en-suite to take a hot shower before bed.

Chapter Two

Preston

Snowflake is a quaint, small town with a lot of potential. It was like a ghost town when I arrived. It seemed I had arrived at just the right time. Of course, the locals didn't like me coming into their territory. There were those that accepted the changes, but there were more that opposed them. I don't know why, considering any changes to this town were being made for the good. I didn't want to walk in here and tear the place down and start again. My grandfather may have been that kind of man, but I am not him. Most people didn't believe me until I showed them what I had to give.

But there's one resident of this town, one small business owner that has resisted my help time and time again. She's stubborn, set in her ways, sees me as some kind of heartless monster. I think she thinks I'm the Grinch who stole Christmas, which is an unfair comparison. I only want the best for all the stores here, for their owners and staff, and for the residents of Snowflake in general. I need to make Aneurin Mackenzie see that I am not a wolf in sheep's clothing.

Usually, I wouldn't care what women think of me, but she's not just any woman. She's a woman who's gone toe-to-toe with me on several occasions and has stood her ground. She's a woman who really holds her own and doesn't bow down to anyone. I guess you could say that her nature appeals to me. She's the opposite of the submissive women I usually meet. The ones who would do anything and everything I ask. I say "jump" and they ask how high.

Typically, it's always been the submissive ones that I have been attracted to. I can bend them to my will. But Aneurin is intriguing and I want to know her better. I want to help her grow her business—that's what I'm here to do for the town, after all—but I also want to know what makes her tick. I want to know how to get under her skin the way she has done with me.

I didn't come to this town looking for a relationship, I'm not actually a "relationship" kind of guy. I prefer to keep it casual and the women I have relations with understand that. They know where they stand. However, Aneurin has me tangled up in knots. I want what I can't have.

Aneurin Mackenzie is beautiful—her dark hair flowing in gentle waves, eyes a stunning green that seem to darken depending on her mood. They go a really dark hue when she's mad. I'd know, considering how many times I've made her mad. She doesn't wear heavy makeup, unlike most women I know. Instead she looks like she wears a little mascara and lip gloss: the natural look. That lip gloss—it gets me hard just thinking of the scent of it combined with the scent of her shampoo and perfume.

She's sexy as hell when she gets angry, such as when I call her Aneurin instead of Nye, unlike everyone else. It's a beautiful name, so I don't like to shorten it. Plus, I like seeing her eyes flash and her nostrils flare when I call her by her full name. I like a feisty woman with a lot of sass. Who knew? I sure didn't.

If I had to say I have a specific type, I'd say blonde hair, blue eyes and legs that go on for miles. Aneurin is everything that hasn't been my type until the day I moved here to Snowflake. Damn her for burying herself under my skin like an itch I need to scratch. Maybe if I slept with her, it would get her out of my system. The only trouble is, she isn't attracted to me. Trust me to want the one girl in town who won't fall at my feet.

I don't know why she won't submit. I mean, I'm tall, have dark hair, and brown eyes that I've been complimented on too many times to count. I'm good looking, dress well … I'm the epitome of the whole "tall, dark and handsome" thing. How can she not be even a little attracted to me? Plus, I drive a fucking Bugatti Veyron, who wouldn't be impressed at that? I have more money than I know what to do with. I usually splash it out on extravagant things like my collection of expensive watches and suits. I thought women liked the whole suited and booted look. Goodness knows you'd never find me in a pair of jeans and a t-shirt. My idea of casual is not wearing a suit jacket or waistcoat and maybe losing the tie. But, at the very least, I always wear a shirt and suit trousers.

My phone dings with an incoming text, so I slip it from my pocket and read:

Jack: Are we going out tonight?

I contemplate saying no because I have so much paperwork to get through and it's already early evening.

Another text chimes:

Jack: We should get shit-faced. I'm totally up for that! Whiskey on you though, dude. You're the one with the cushy bank balance, after all.

I laugh. My best friend is a total tool. He knows I can't resist the temptation of a bottle of twenty-five-year-old Macallan. But he also knows, just like I do, that he can't afford my expensive tastes.

Preston: I don't know, man. Loads of paperwork to get through.

I cast my eye over the rather large piles of paper on my desk. I itch to get rid of it all. I want a paperless office. Not just because it's better for the environment—although that is a factor—but because I like clean lines. I don't like mess. Even tidied up, this shit still looks a mess.

My phone chimes again.

Jack: Dude, paperwork will still be there tomorrow. Come on out and let loose. Pull a blondie with big boobs and a great ass. Take her home, show her a good time. Release some of this pent-up shit you got going on.

Trust Jack to think sex is the answer to everything. But he has a point about releasing my pent-up aggression. I either punch the shit out of the bag in the gym, or I take my pick of women and let her help ease the tension. But I don't want that tonight. Evelyn Mackenzie and I had a meeting with the mayor earlier about the Christmas decorations in town and the lighting of the tree. They want me to come down from my ivory tower and be at the ceremony for my first Christmas here. Talking to Evelyn always makes me think of her daughter, and when that happens some random chick from the bar just won't cut it.

I tap out a reply:

Preston: It's a no to the woman, but I'll come out for an hour or two. Just give me 30 minutes to make a couple of phone calls. I'll meet you in Mistletoe & Wine. Damn, this town has some stupid names for places!

Jack: It sure does, but then the town itself has a name synonymous with Christmas. I don't know, maybe it's rubbing off on me. It's quirky. Can you hurry up and come and pay for this whiskey? Not sure I can afford the stuff you drink, so I'll stick with the cheap stuff … for now.

I'll get the barman to crack a Macallan open when you arrive.

Trust him. He knows I'll pick up the tab and I really hate the cheap stuff. It has an almost chemical-like burn, whereas the stuff I drink is smooth as it warms its way down your throat.

Preston: Look at you with your big words. Did someone eat a dictionary for breakfast? Cool your jets and I'll meet you there soon.

I see three dots bouncing, meaning he's replying.

Jack: Suck a dick, man. I know big words, just like you. I just don't need to use them all the time.

Laughing, I slip my phone back in my pocket and pick up the receiver on my desk to make a couple of quick business calls that I had intended to make tomorrow. That way, at least if I have a banging head in the morning, I'll have a head start on the day.

***

I reach the bar and Jack swivels on his stool to face me.

"About you time you got here, my throat feels like it's on fire. I've told the barman to open a bottle of the good stuff, he just needs your credit card to open a tab."

I pass my card over to the barman, he swipes it and hands it back along with an open bottle of whiskey and two glasses.

Jack and I sit and shoot the breeze for a while; I need to unwind and stop stressing about the amount of work I have to do. That's the good thing about my best friend, he knows my grandfather was an ass, and that it all went to shit when my father passed away so young and I had to take on the family business. It's not a job I ever wanted to do. It didn't fit in with my life plan at all. Why did I have to be an only child, so the mantle got passed to me? If only my father hadn't passed away. He was the one who had the head for the family business. Yeah, I'd gone to business school, but I didn't earn my degree so that I could follow in their footsteps. I'd wanted to be my own man and start my own business venture. None of that mattered when it came to the crunch though. My mother told me I had no choice because she didn't know what she was doing and if I didn't step into the breach the family business would fold. Good guilt trip, Mom.

After the fourth glass of whiskey, I spot a gorgeous brunette standing across the bar from me. Her green gaze collides with mine and it feels like my heart has stopped. She breaks my gaze and I release a breath I didn't even realize I was holding. My heart thunders in my chest, feeling like it'll break free any moment. My cock gets hard just seeing her in that emerald green mini-dress. The material clings to her like a second skin and I find myself jealous of a dress. I want to be molded to her curves in the same way. I want to touch her, tease her, taste her—every inch of her. I want her to succumb to her needs and submit to me. Or do I want her to dominate me? Either way, she's like a match, where I am a tank of gas. Together, we'd be combustible. I'm damn sure of it.

Summoning the courage, I hold my shoulders back and my head up as I walk in her direction. Jack calls something to me, but I don't catch it; my focus is purely on Aneurin.

There's a blonde woman dressed in red standing next to her. She might be my usual type, if I hadn't got a thing about this particular brunette. Long blonde hair left loose in waves, brown eyes that look like she could give you the perfect "puppy dog eye" look. Her red dress is mid-thigh length and made of some sort of floaty material. There's no doubt she's an attractive woman, but I'm zeroing in on a woman in green.

Pulling up short, I think what I'm about to say. I actually have no idea. My mind has gone blank like someone has erased everything, including my own name.

Up close, the dress she's wearing looks more like it's painted on. It clings to all the right places. A generous amount of cleavage on show, but not enough to be indecent. Her legs go on for miles and end in green high heels that make my cock throb as I think about her wearing nothing except those shoes.

The blonde whispers something to Aneurin and she looks my way. Her smile could light the whole room. Her perfect white teeth make me zero in on her mouth. Her lips are painted a soft pink. I'm not sure if it's her usual lip gloss, but they look as soft and kissable as they do whenever I see her.

"Preston," she says and gives me a small nod. Her chest blushes with a slight rosy glow that rushes up to her cheeks.

"Aneurin," I reply with my trademark smirk.

"How many times do I have to tell you; my name is Nye."

"I'm sorry, darling. It's a beautiful name and I like using it."

"It's so formal. Only my mother and you ever address me as such. It's a pain in the ass."

"I'm sorry, Aneurin. I don't mean to be a pain in the ass."

I shrug and grin at her. She blushes again at the double meaning behind my words. Her blonde friend nudges her with her elbow.

"Sorry, Paisley, this is Preston. Preston, this is my assistant at *Style in Snowflake*, Paisley."

Paisley holds her hand out for me to shake, so I take her palm in mine and shake it firmly.

"It's nice to meet you at last," she says. "Nye has told me about you."

"I'm sure she told you all good things, right?!"

"Umm…" she blushes, and I can tell Aneurin has told her I'm an asshole.

It's true; I am an asshole. I get what I want, when I want it. I'm not used to waiting. In this case, all I want to do is help Aneurin build her business up to attract more customers, people from out of town, get the business online and attract people via social media—well, that may not be *all* I want, but it is in the business sense of things. I don't know why she's so resistant to my plans.

"Don't worry, I don't bite. I'm not the monster under the bed that I'm sure people think I am."

I flash her my megawatt grin, hoping to win her over. Maybe she can help me find my way to Aneurin, in the business sense. I don't think she'd exactly be up for helping me get to know her boss in the carnal sense. But I'll take what I can get.

"I'm sure you're not," she says softly.

"Is there something I can do for you, Preston?" Aneurin asks, a little annoyance in her tone.

"I just wanted to come and say hello. I'm still getting to know people here and finding my way around."

"Nye could help you get to know people. She's lived in Snowflake all her life. There isn't anyone here that she doesn't know," Paisley says as she looks between the two of us.

"Oh yes, I'll be his personal tour guide," Aneurin says with more than a touch of sarcasm.

"Don't be snippy, Nye, it doesn't suit you," Paisley says.

"Sarcasm is my second language," Aneurin replies before taking a sip of her cocktail.

I don't know what she's drinking, but it's pink and frilly. Totally girly. It suits her.

"I'll leave you girls to it," I say, second-guessing myself for ever venturing to come and speak to her.

"Don't go," Paisley chimes in before I turn on my heel.

Aneurin sighs and puts her drink back on the bar.

"I didn't mean to be rude. Pull up a stool and I'll get you a drink," she relents, looking directly into my eyes.

"I'll get us a round in," I say as I pull up an empty barstool.

"Don't worry about me, I should be getting home. Early start in the morning," Paisley says as she places her empty glass on the bar.

"Don't leave on my account."

"Oh, I'm not. I need to get a good night's sleep."

Paisley shrugs on her coat and kisses Aneurin on the cheek, whispering something to her before she bids us both goodnight.

"Looks like it's just the two of us," Aneurin says in what I could be forgiven for thinking is a lusty tone of voice.

I look back to see where Jack is and notice he's no longer sitting at the bar. I pull out my phone and send him a quick text. He replies that he decided to leave me and Aneurin to it. He'd also seen "the blonde" as he puts it, leaving the bar and thought he'd go and chat to her. I tap out a text wishing him luck and telling him her name.

Sitting opposite Aneurin, I'm hypnotized by her green eyes. They're framed by long, thick lashes and are quite possibly the most beautiful eyes I've ever seen. As I look at her, her tongue darts out to wet her bottom lip and I have to bite my lip to stop myself from leaning in to lick the same path as her tongue.

"So, how's life here in the small town of Snowflake?" she asks me.

"I'm settling in … I think. I still don't really know my way around. I spend too much time in the office and at meetings to actually get out and look around the town."

"Well, I know I was a sarcastic cow before, but actually I would be a pretty good tour guide of this place. Paisley was right. I was born here, and I'll probably die here. It's all I've known for thirty-one years."

She doesn't look a day over twenty-five and although women generally like to be complimented, I'm not so sure I could buy Aneurin's affection with words.

"It's a beautiful little place and the tree in the center of town makes it feel very festive. I saw it on the way in and I've been asked to light the tree by the mayor."

"You have? I thought she was doing that herself as she's new here."

"She asked me, but I haven't agreed … yet. Do you think I ought to?"

"Unless you're Ebenezer Scrooge..."

"I have no problem with Christmas. I'm just not sure I should be the one to light the tree considering I'm new to town. Seems that's exactly why the mayor wants me to, but that's one reason I'm not sure I should."

"It's a way to get to know the people in town. Everyone comes out to see the lights come on."

The barman comes over and I order a glass of Macallan and whatever it is Aneurin is drinking.

"I guess..."

I trail off as I take in her long legs as she crosses one over the other. The hem of her dress rides up and I have to remind myself to be a gentleman and not look.

We talk for a while longer before Aneurin says she has to call it a night. I have work early too, but I'd much rather spend more time in her company.

She orders a cab via the app on her phone and I escort her outside to wait. I see she hasn't brought a coat, so I shrug out of my suit jacket and drape it around her shoulders. Smiling at me shyly, she thanks me for the gesture.

The lamppost casts a flattering glow and I can't help but look her over from head to toe. She could quite possibly be the most attractive woman I have ever met. Her hair blows in the gentle breeze and her green eyes are like the prettiest, rarest gems in the world.

Any other time, I'd be trying to guess why she isn't putty in my hands, why she isn't coming home with me for the night—just a hookup, a night of fun that wouldn't be repeated—but Nye is different. I prefer to call her by her full name, but she insisted that if we are to be friends, I am not to call her Aneurin because that's an annoyance reserved only for her mother.

Why is she different? I can't quite put my finger on a defining reason, I guess there are several. If I were to list them, I guess I'd say it's because she's unlike the random women that I normally meet. Maybe that's because I'm seeing her through different eyes. I normally look for fun, flirty, bubbly, vivacious women, but even though Nye is all of those things and more, she's not as vapid and vacuous as them. There's something that separates her and puts her in a different class—one I've never seen any other woman in before—that makes me see and treat her differently. I want to respect her and gain her respect too. We didn't start off on the best footing, but I want to change that. I guess you could say I breezed into town on my high horse—a bit like my grandfather would have done in his day—and tried to get her to adapt to all the changes I anticipated making to her business.

It's not that I want to change her boutique itself, nor the beautiful women's clothing that they sell. She has a great USP—unique selling point—and that's done her well this far. Her style is somewhat different to other clothing stores. But it could be so much more. If she allowed me to create a website for *Style in Snowflake*, to advertise on social media and get the word out, her business could grow exponentially. The only problem is, she won't listen to me and I don't know how to change that.

Her cab pulls up and I act like the gentleman my mother brought me up to be as I open the passenger door for her. She thanks me and flashes me that beautiful smile of hers. There's something about a woman with a gorgeous smile that makes my knees weak. Her lips are full and look like they'd be soft to touch and caress with my own. I know that won't happen, but a boy can dream.

"Goodnight, Preston, and thank you for the drinks … and the company."

"Goodnight, Nye. Safe journey home."

I close the door behind her and watch as the cab pulls away. I can't tell if she's looking back, but I stay and watch as it drives off into the distance.

I call myself a cab and stand outside in the crisp night air, taking deep, calming breaths to try and get my heartbeat back into its regular rhythm. My heart beats and my palms get clammy like a teenage boy whenever I am around Aneurin. I wish I could figure out why.

Chapter Three

Nye

Last night was fun. I can't stop thinking about how different Preston was when he wasn't in his work environment. The way he looked at me like he wanted to devour me made the hairs on the backs of my arms stand on end along with those at the nape of my neck. But it had to have been my imagination; maybe it was the amount of alcohol I'd consumed. A man like Preston Wolfric Fitzgerald III doesn't date women like me. I'm too ... normal.

He probably has a Rolodex full of women that he can call up for a booty call or whatever people call it these days. They're probably all tall, blonde and curvy with a generous amount of cleavage. He likely only dates highly intelligent women, something I'm not. I mean, I'm not dumb, but I'm not in the same class as the women he dates. They'll all have money and come from different backgrounds to me. They probably attended Ivy League schools, something I could never afford to do. My father has money, but his business didn't really take off until I was already old enough to work for myself, so he couldn't pay my way through school.

Instead, I worked my ass off at a normal public school here in Snowflake. I took business classes and got my degree. That was when I decided I didn't want to work for somebody else. I wanted to be my own boss and I worked damn hard to make that fantasy a reality.

My father helped me with a business loan to get *Style in Snowflake* off the ground and I paid him back in monthly installments. When I'd finished, I felt like the store was really my own.

With so many big clothing stores in neighboring towns, I knew I couldn't compete. So, I decided not to. I took my own quirky style and molded the store around that. Of course, I couldn't be sure it was going to work, but it went better than I could have hoped. It worked so well I had to take on an assistant and I knew Paisley hated her job, so I asked her to come and work with me; she jumped at the chance and has never looked back.

The first time I saw Preston, he walked in with his shoulders back and his head held high. He tried to talk me into all sorts of things I didn't want and wouldn't be reasoned with. He gave me his business card in case I changed my mind and, whilst normally I wouldn't have minded, even his business card was flashy. It was made of titanium and highly polished, just like its owner, and I wanted to throw the damn thing in the bin. The only reason I kept it was because titanium isn't recyclable. Damn him and his flash suits and business cards. He really seemed like a douche. Paisley and I had talked about it afterward because she hadn't been there to meet him and, as she looked at the metal in her hand, she got frustrated that she couldn't just crumple it up and throw it in the trash. So even she wasn't impressed with him and she hadn't even met him.

But last night she'd been more than impressed with him, mentioning how handsome he was, how gorgeous his bone structure was … her tongue damn near rolled out of her head and tripped her up. Of course, she's right. An impressive bone structure, a chiseled jawline, chocolate brown eyes and a body that looks like it was made for sin … damn her for pointing that out and damn him for being so sexy. I need to get him out of my head.

I jump into the shower and program it to beat down on me. It feels like tiny bullets all over my skin and is a little hotter than normal because I feel the need to wash Preston right out of my head.

I picture him in my mind—that sinfully sexy body in an expensive, tailored suit … his blemish free skin and his big, strong hands … I want him to touch me in places I haven't been touched for a long time. If he was here, he'd take his time exploring every inch of my skin with his fingers, then follow that trail with his tongue. He'd take my nipples in his deft hands, making them pebble against his skin. His full, soft-looking lips would slant down over mine and claim them in a slow, languorous kiss. Then it would become more urgent, his tongue dancing with mine. He'd wrap my hair around his fist and pull it back to expose my neck, place featherlight kisses down to the hollow of my throat and through the valley between my breasts…then he would take my nipple in his mouth and gently nip it between his teeth before moving to the other one and paying it the same attention…

Pulling myself from my own thoughts, I realize I'm breathing heavily. My eyes feel heavy and my head is full of lust-fueled thoughts, but what's more is my abdomen feels coiled, ready to explode with the orgasm I'm dying for Preston to give me. Why can't he look at me as more than a pawn in his game for getting Snowflake on the map once and for all?

***

Ready for the day ahead, I grab my bag—making sure I have my phone and car keys—then I lock up and head to work.

Paisley has already opened up and greets me with a smile.

"Morning, boss," she says, sounding chipper.

I guess she didn't drink as much as I did last night. Although I wasn't drunk, I did wake with a bit of a headache.

She doesn't know it, but I won't be her boss much longer if she accepts my Christmas present.

"Morning, Paisley."

I hang my coat in the back before realizing that it isn't my coat at all. I'd grabbed the first one off the rack this morning, which I am now shocked to see is Preston's jacket from last night.

Remembering how much of a gentleman he was to loan it to me while I waited for a cab makes me smile and I feel a heat rise to my cheeks. I'm probably a little flushed looking, having momentarily been taken back to my thoughts of how dangerously sexy Preston is.

Making a cup of coffee for the two of us gives me a chance to cool off and to search our little kitchenette for the business card I had tucked away in a drawer. I find it easily, then slip my phone out of my bag and send a text:

Nye: Hi Preston, it's Nye. It seems I still have your jacket from last night. I'm so sorry, I hadn't meant to take it home. Is there somewhere we could meet when I get off work so I can return it?

It takes only a few moments to get a response:

Preston: I won't lie, it slipped my mind entirely until I realized I didn't have it when I got home and if you put your hand in the pocket, you'll find my car keys. Obviously not my finest moment, as I had to get a cab to work today.

Damn. I slip my hand into the pocket and discover he's telling the truth. Now I feel extra guilty for him having to get a cab to work. I quickly type out a reply:

Nye: I'm so sorry, Preston. I can drive to your office and return your jacket and keys. Give me around half an hour and I'll be there.

I slip out of the kitchenette and hand Paisley her coffee, explaining what's happened. I quickly gulp back my own coffee as I hear my phone chime with what I assume is Preston's reply:

Preston: Don't worry, I can get a cab from work later on and meet you to retrieve them.

Nye: No, I insist. I don't want to leave you all day without your car.

Paisley tells me not to worry, she'll hold the fort while I'm gone. I slip out to my car with Preston's jacket in hand. Lifting it, I inhale his intoxicating scent. I'm not sure what it is, but it smells exquisite.

I hear my phone chime as I put his jacket on the passenger seat. I read another reply:

Preston: Honestly, Aneurin, it's fine. I can cope for one day. I only have a few meetings and I can get a cab.

I know he's got the money to get a cab or two—probably even a chauffeur-driven limousine if we're being honest—but that isn't the point.

I type out a short reply, then get in the car ready to drive to his office:

Nye: See you in twenty minutes.

Pulling out onto the street, I ignore my phone when it begins to ring. I'm nothing if not adamant.

***

When I arrive at Preston's office, I pull my car into a space and grab his jacket, making sure his keys are definitely in the pocket.

I walk up to the door and press the button for the intercom. I am greeted by a friendly female voice. I tell her who I am, and she buzzes me in.

The reception of his office building is impressive. High ceilings, a room fronted by glass, a reception desk that looks like black granite and chrome ... it all works beautifully together. Then I notice the chandelier high above my head and, although I think it's an odd choice for an office, it doesn't actually look as strange as one might think it ought to.

I walk over to the pretty red-haired receptionist and she tells me she has alerted Mr. Fitzgerald to my presence and he will be with me shortly.

Sitting in a gorgeous leather armchair, I look around at the furniture and see that somebody really does have excellent taste. It all reeks of having money, yet it feels comfortable and all I want to do is sink into the chair, pull my feet up beneath me and read a good book with a cup of hot chocolate.

Preston walks out of a door to my left and it feels like all the air is sucked from the room. He looks strikingly handsome in a tailored grey suit, which he's paired with a crisp white shirt and a black tie. My eyes are drawn to his as if by a magnet. The smile on his face is contagious and I feel myself grin in response.

"Aneurin, good to see you."

His Hollywood smile dazzles me and momentarily clouds my thoughts. For a second, I forget why I'm here.

"Aneurin?" he makes my name sound like a question.

I shake my head, hoping to clear my thoughts.

"Sorry, Preston. I was … admiring … the décor."

He gives me an impish grin as if he can tell that wasn't what I was doing at all "Thank you. I like to think this place feels like a mixture of business and pleasure. Those comfortable armchairs, for example. They're almost built for one purpose."

"And what would that be?" I ask, curious to know what goes through that beautiful mind of his.

"Settling in with a good book and a mug of cocoa," he replies.

"But if that's the case, why have them here?"

"Because I like them and because I can. Do I need another reason?"

His gorgeous mouth looks soft and kissable as it quirks into another smile. I'm pretty sure that's all he does—smile. But I'm sure there are plenty of other things he could do with that mouth of his, although I dare not allow my mind to go there. I'm here to return his jacket and keys, nothing more.

"Of course you don't. I like the décor. It's very modern, all clean lines and perfect symmetry. Tell me, though, the chandelier…"

I wait for a moment as he gazes up at it without saying anything.

"It was my grandmother's. She died some time ago and bequeathed me the house and all her possessions. I always loved this chandelier as a child, she knew that. I have it here because my grandmother was an amazing woman and I like the reminder of her every day."

"I'm sorry to hear she passed. My own grandmother died when I was a teenager. It's nice to have a little something of theirs to remember them by, isn't it?"

His eyes mist over as he glances towards it once more. I can tell he was close to his grandmother just by the look etched on his face. It's one of sadness and loss, yet happiness and good memories. I feel the same whenever I think of my own grandparents. They were pretty amazing people and there isn't a day that goes by when I don't think of them.

I don't want to interrupt his reverie, but I must get back to the store. I left Paisley on her own and, though she can cope, I feel bad for leaving her to it.

I clear my throat and Preston's eyes meet my own again. Will there ever be a time when I am not drawn to those eyes? They look like pools of liquid chocolate at first, but the closer I look, I see that around the pupil they are more amber with little flecks of gold.

"Sorry, I was lost in my own thoughts there for a moment," he says.

"I know the feeling. Anyway, I'm sorry but I have to be going, I've left Paisley alone in the store. Here's your jacket. The car keys are in the pocket. Again, I'm really sorry."

"Thank you," he says, taking the jacket and brushing his fingers against mine, causing the hairs on the back of my arm to stand on end. "I'll grab a cab home and fetch the car. It will be easier than having to get cabs to my appointments all day. I really appreciate you coming all the way over here."

"I can drop you home on my way back to the store."

I don't know why I just said that and I immediately mentally chastise myself.

"Oh no, you've done enough, and I've taken you away from your job for long enough. I don't want to impose on you any further."

Maybe I offered him a lift because subconsciously I want to spend a bit more time with him, but he obviously doesn't want to have to spend any more time with me.

"I really wouldn't mind. After all, I am the reason you're in this predicament in the first place. But if you want to wait for the small cab service from the next town over, that's your prerogative."

I didn't mean to come across snappy, but my tone of voice wasn't as pleasant as it could have been.

"I only declined your offer because I don't want to take you away from your job. But I can tell I've offended you and I'm sorry for that. It was unintentional, I assure you."

His face is crestfallen, and I can see only one way to fix it.

"Come on, get in my car and I'll drop you home."

I smile at him—hoping it comes across as sincere. It coaxes a small smile from him in return and he is hot on my heels as I turn to leave.

"Nice car," he says as he lets out a low whistle of appreciation.

He can obviously afford to drive whatever the hell he wants, but that doesn't mean he can't appreciate the beauty that is my Mercedes E-class. Most men know a good car when they see one, even if it's not as amazing as the one they drive.

The drive to his house is full of inane chatter about anything and nothing. He tells me he's an only child, but his best friend Jack is like a brother. It's clear he loves his mother from the way he talks about her. He says how much it hurt him and his mother when his father died young. He loved him and idolized him, how it should have been him taking over the family business. He tells me his grandfather, however, was an ass—arrogant, cocky, got what he wanted, when he wanted it. I want to laugh, to tell him that's how I saw him when he came to town, but I don't want to insult him. Truth is, he still comes across as a bit of an arrogant, cocky guy who is used to getting his own way. But now, as I get to know little things about him, it's like cracks are beginning to appear in his façade. Maybe he's not as much of a jerk as people have him down as being.

"You have great taste in music," he remarks as Depeche Mode play on my iPod.

"Thanks. I get the feeling you're shocked about that," I joke.

"I don't know, I just had you down as being more of a country music girl."

"Oh, well, you have that right. Lady Antebellum, Carrie Underwood, Luke Bryan, Brad Paisley and, of course, the king of country, Garth Brooks. I love them all. I've been to tons of gigs. But I have an appreciation for music in general. If I like a song, I like it. I'm not fussed what genre it falls under."

"Why is it I can just picture you in cowboy boots complete with spurs and a Stetson?"

"Well, I have a confession ... I do own boots and a Stetson."

I can feel his stare burning holes in the side of my head as I drive. I imagine he's trying to picture me dressed for a country gig. I own the most gorgeous pair of boots, they're probably about ten years old now, but I won't replace them because they're comfortable. I don't see them as "old", I see them as "broken in". And my jet-black Stetson is something I truly love. My grandmother bought it for me, so it has sentimental value too. It was one of the last gifts she gave me before she passed away.

"Turn left here," Preston says, somehow feeling closer to me than I thought he was.

I do as he instructed and that's when I see it. My breath catches in my throat as I look up and see the impressive building in front of me. There's a tall, black wrought-iron gate set in stone pillars at the bottom of the driveway. Looking beyond, it looks like it has its own courtyard. The house itself looks Edwardian. One of the upper windows has a small Juliet balcony. The trees surround the property as if they are shielding it, like it was built to be imposing and yet fit in with the countryside at the same time. I've never seen anything quite like it.

"Punch in the code 1608," Preston says, jolting me back to myself.

I enter the code on the panel and the electric gates open slowly. As we drive up the driveway, I see the courtyard and the surrounding greenery. If I had a dream home, this would be it.

Having grown up in Snowflake, I remember this house in the back of my mind. But it wasn't like this back then. Sure, the house itself was mostly the same but some additions have been made that make it more beautiful, yet it looks like the builder was told to be sensitive to the original features.

The house looked older in my memory. It seems that some things probably had to be replaced and updated before Preston moved in. He must have also installed the gates and the security cameras I can see. The cameras aren't obvious and in your face, but I notice even the smallest of details most of the time.

I park the car on the courtyard next to his Bugatti. It really is a very sleek and sexy car. I've always said if money was no object, I'd buy a Bugatti or an Aston Martin; the DB9 or the Vanquish.

It feels like I'm drooling over Preston's car and his beautiful home, so I turn and look at him. He's so close I could kiss him. It makes me wonder if he's a good kisser. I'm sure he is. I'm sure he's a man who knows exactly what he's doing in every area of his life. His eyes hold mine and I'm sure I see them twinkle with mirth, like he knows exactly what I'm thinking.

As he leans closer, he seems to inhale deeply before kissing my cheek lightly.

"Thank you for dropping me home. It wasn't necessary, but I appreciate it all the same."

"No problem."

He opens his car door and gets out. Suddenly I feel bereft; the loss of him next to me feels tangible. The warmth of his body is gone, but his scent lingers. I close my eyes, inhale it and store it in my memory.

He walks around the front of the car and he comes to a stop at my window.

"Thanks again. If you're around this weekend, Jack and I will be at the bar. I owe you a drink at the very least for the trouble you've gone to for me."

"Oh please, if it wasn't for me, you wouldn't have been without your keys and none of this would have happened."

"I'm glad it did," he says as he walks to his car.

Cryptic much? Why would he be glad it happened? I've inconvenienced him. Men. Typically hard creatures to understand at the best of times.

***

"He's so gorgeous. You should definitely be at the bar this weekend. I'll be your wing-woman," Paisley says like an overenthusiastic puppy.

"Maybe. Now can we actually get on with some work?" I ask as I finish the takeout coffee I bought us on my way back to the store.

I told her all about my encounter with Preston and of course she picked up on the vibes I was obviously exuding. Normally, I like to play my cards close to my chest, but Paisley is my closest friend, so she knows all my "tells" that show how I really feel.

Paisley's idea of getting back to work is going around the store to find the perfect outfit for me to wear this weekend. She says it needs to be conservative, yet provocative. I didn't think we had anything in the store that fits that description, but she finds something and refuses to show me. Typical Paisley. She's trouble when she sets her mind to something. I just leave her to it.

After closing time, Paisley tells me she's booked me into the salon for a mani-pedi, as well as nail extensions and getting my hair done. She says she'll close the store on Saturday, so I can make it to my appointment. I pout like a child for all of about five minutes, but the schooled features I wear on the outside are a stark contrast to the butterflies in my stomach.

I try telling her I don't want the appointment, but she won't hear it and tells me she'll even pay if it'll shut me up. Knowing how much her salary is, I wouldn't dream of letting her pay, so I tell her I'll go just to shut her up.

Chapter Four

Preston

I spend longer than usual getting ready, making sure I look good, just in case Nye turns up tonight. I'm really hoping she does, but nothing was set in stone.

I've wanted to text her since the other day when she dropped me home, but I haven't known what to say. I wanted to tell Jack not to come, I wanted it to be a date with Nye, but I also didn't want to rush things with her. She's only just starting to seem like she actually likes me.

She spent so long butting heads with me when I first arrived in Snowflake. She refused to listen to my business ideas and she always acted like she thinks I'm a jerk. But recently, her mood seems to have shifted, hinting at her liking me more than she did then.

I'm not even sure whether she'll be here tonight, but I'm sitting at the bar with Jack, hoping she'll walk in any minute. The manager of Mistletoe & Wine seems to have gone all out with the festive decorations. I keep forgetting it's almost Christmas. It reminds me I don't even have a tree at home. Honestly, my house feels kind of empty. It's a big place for a single guy to rattle around in. It's more like a family home, but it was so beautiful that I couldn't not buy it. Maybe one day I'll settle down and have children, but I refuse to entertain the idea right now. I'm far too busy. My mind has always been more focused on work, maybe to my detriment. I guess I'm a chip off the old block when it comes to my grandfather. He stepped up and acted like a father-figure when my father died. He was always consumed with work. Sure, he married my grandmother, but that was before his business took off and I have a feeling that if those two events had happened the other way around, maybe he wouldn't have married at all.

Jack and I are shooting the breeze and drinking my favorite whiskey when a figure appears in the doorway. She's wearing a blue dress that dips into a V in the valley between her breasts. Her cleavage is accentuated but doesn't show too much skin because of the lace that runs along that V line.

My eyes roam her body from head to toe. The blue material clings to her curves like a second skin. Her hair is down one side in a kind of plait. With soft, understated makeup, apart from a smoky color that makes her green eyes really stand out and a red lip that looks seductive as hell, she looks like a temptress; a goddess carved from marble made to call to me like a siren.

Her legs seem to go on forever and I can't help but notice how toned and shapely they are. She's wearing silver heels and I notice a silver clutch in her hand that matches them. She doesn't look my way, which only gives me longer to appreciate her without her noticing.

Men are looking at her in a way that makes me want to rip out their eyeballs and shove them down their throats. I want to go all caveman—pick her up over my shoulder and drag her back to my cave so that it's only the two of us.

As I watch her walk to the bar, I notice that the back of the dress dips dangerously low. It only just meets the base of her spine. My cock twitches as I imagine reaching out to touch her creamy skin. I don't know how it's possible here in Snowflake, but she has a beautiful sun-kissed glow to her skin that I can tell is natural rather than a spray tan.

It's funny, the women I usually find myself attracted to are diametrically opposed to this intoxicating beauty in front of me. This woman is all-natural beauty, not fake like most of my exes—if you can even call them that. I normally say they are a fling and nothing more. It's never serious with anyone. I don't have room in my life for a woman. But I'm starting to feel like I could make room for one woman in particular.

I want to go straight over to her, but I don't want to seem too eager. I nearly kissed her in the car the other day; the only thing that stopped me was a sudden loss of courage, so I ended up kissing her cheek instead. Normally I am pretty cocky, and I get what I want by just going for it. But Nye is different. She makes me lose myself. She makes me want to be different. To be better. For her.

Minutes pass as I watch her interact with Paisley, who also looks pretty in a black dress. I'm quite sure Jack will be making an excuse to go and talk to her at some point.

The song in the background changes to one I'm sure Nye loves, and she takes Paisley's hand and walks to the small makeshift dance floor. The two dance and I am hypnotized. I'm not sure if she's dancing seductively on purpose or if it's my imagination.

Hips swaying to the beat and arms in the air, her body moves in ways I want to feel rather than just see.

"Blue Dress" by Depeche Mode continues to play, but the words are lost on me as I am too focused on Nye in her little blue dress. She's sex personified, and I don't think she even realizes it or the effect she's having on me.

I look around and see too many eyes on her. I want to claim her as mine right in front of them so they know not to look, let alone touch. But Nye would probably slap me for marking my territory when it isn't even mine to mark. She isn't mine and I have to remember that. However hard I try to remind myself of the facts, she's in my veins and I can't get her out. She's the sun to my moon, the soft to my hard, the opposite of everything I ever thought I wanted, but everything I've come to realize I need. How am I falling when we're worlds apart? She doesn't even think of me in the same way, but I want to make her. To persuade her I would be good for her just like she'd be good for me. I just don't know how because my usual confidence has fled, leaving me feeling like a teenage boy who doesn't know what to do with the beautiful woman he sees before him.

The song changes to something I recognize as a country song, but the title escapes me. It talks about being just the two of us, the rhythm of her heartbeat. I notice as emerald green eyes lock onto mine. She knows I'm here. Knows I'm watching her every move. Her body moves seductively and, this time, I know it's not my imagination. She beckons me over with a crook of her finger and a salacious smile. She's a siren calling to me and I am helpless as I get down from my stool at the bar and walk towards her. She's in control of me and I choose to surrender to it rather than being my usual dominant self.

Her back is turned to me and I want more than ever to touch her soft skin. I refrain from doing so, instead placing my hands on her hips, lightly at first to give her a chance to object. When she doesn't push me away, I hold her more firmly and move my body in sync with hers as "Out of Nowhere Girl" begins to play. The lyrics make me wonder if this song wasn't written about me and Nye.

As the song ends, Nye turns in my arms and looks up at me from under those long lashes. If I'm not mistaken, I see a hint of lust in her gaze. My gaze flickers to her lips, soft, painted red and oh-so-kissable … but I don't kiss her. I want her to come to me. I want her to make the first move so that I know I'm not imagining whatever this is between us. To my disappointment, she doesn't move to kiss me. Instead, she takes my hand and walks in the direction of the bar.

"Hi," she says on a gentle sigh as we reach the bar.

"Hi."

"If I'm not mistaken, you said you owe me a drink," she says as she takes a seat and calls the bartender over.

"What can I get you? Wine? Prosecco?"

"How about whiskey. Neat. No ice. Don't dilute my drink, that's sacrilegious."

Her face transforms as a smile lights up her eyes.

"My kind of girl," I reply, unable to come up with anything else to say.

I definitely feel like a teenager with his first crush. Nye takes my breath away and with it, all coherent thought.

***

The guy at the cab firm said it would be about twenty minutes before Nye's cab would arrive. She took my hand and walked us out into the crisp night air. I'm leaning my back against the brick wall with one knee bent and my foot flat on the wall. I've loosened my tie and opened the top button of my shirt. Even when I'm going out with Jack, I still tend to dress the way I do at the office.

Jack and Paisley left a little while ago. He'd asked her if she'd like to go for something to eat and she'd been only too happy to agree from what I could see. I was glad because Jack deserves a good woman and because it left me alone with Nye.

We've had a good night. Or at least I have for sure, and I hope Nye has. She's been quiet for the last couple of minutes, as though she has something on her mind. I want to ask, but I don't want to pry. She's making me act in ways I never used to when it came to women. I can't put my finger on it, but she makes me feel different inside.

"Thank you for a good evening, Preston. You're not like I thought you were. I guess I should be less judgmental and more open-minded," Nye says quietly.

I look at her and smile. She really speaks her mind. I like that.

"Sorry, I didn't mean that to sound rude. All I meant was ... well ... I guess at first, I thought you were a little cocky, dominant, power-hungry ... Sorry, I'm really not making it any better, am I? I just ... you're not what I perceived you to be."

"It's okay, I know what you mean. I come across as a confident—and yes, I guess cocky—kind of guy. But that's not all I am, not by a long shot."

I'm silenced when her lips come crashing down over mine.

Her tongue begs for entry to my mouth and I am only too happy to oblige. Our tongues dance together as she grips the front of my jacket, pulling me closer. There isn't room for a breath between us as I turn us around and push her back against the wall. Her lips move from my mouth to my jaw, trailing up to my ear. I can't hide my arousal as she nips my earlobe between her teeth and her breath feels warm against my skin. Hands tangle in my hair, she pulls me closer and her kisses turn more urgent. Her chest rises and falls rapidly, and I can feel her nipples pebble under the thin material covering them.

My hands roam her body and as I brush my thumb over her nipple she gasps and arches her back. I wish we weren't in such a public location, otherwise I'd show her exactly what she's doing to me. Instead, I push my groin against her and she gasps again as she feels the evidence of my attraction to her.

I pull her hair so that she tilts her head and exposes her neck to me. I place featherlight kisses down to the hollow of her throat as my deft fingers play with the material covering her voluptuous breasts. My hand slips underneath the thin material and Nye groans as I find her nipple. She purrs like a kitten as I toy with her. With a knee between her legs, I feel her rub herself against me, trying to gain some friction.

No words are spoken as she brazenly reaches down and cups my erection. She strokes the length of me over my suit trousers. I can't help the throaty moan that escapes me. I want to reach under the hem of her dress and play with her clit, I want to push that detonate button and make her come all over my fingers. But right here is too public for that kind of indecency. I need to take her somewhere more private for something like that. It takes all the strength and restraint I have not to touch her the way she's begging to be touched. She doesn't need to say it; I can read the lust, want and need in her eyes the way I'm pretty sure she can read it in mine.

A car horn sounds, breaking the little bubble we've created for ourselves. I look to see her cab has arrived and realize the driver could have got a good eyeful of us. Too under her spell to care what anyone thinks, least of all a cab driver, I walk her to the door and, knowing the morning will bring more clarity to the situation, I kiss her soft, supple lips like it may be the last time.

Nye breaks the kiss, slides into the cab and sinks into the leather seat. Just as I think she's going to close the door, she crooks her finger at me, beckoning me like she did across the dance floor earlier. I freeze in place momentarily, trying to think this through. I don't want her to wake up full of regret, but I can't deny how much I want her. There's a chemistry between us that I've never felt before. It's like I'm a tank of gas and she's a striking match. Knowing that I'll regret it if I don't go with her—after all, it could be my one and only chance—I get into the cab and give the driver my address.

Nye snuggles into my side and, cloaked in darkness, she traces a finger up and down the length of my erection. My cock throbs, aching for her touch, skin against skin.

If there's no tomorrow and tonight is all we have, I intend to make the most of every moment. I want to make her body come alive with my touch, to feel her as she climaxes again and again. I ache with need for this intoxicating woman and I can't wait to get her into my bed; a place I've imagined her being since the moment we met.

Chapter Five

Nye

The morning after

I don't know what got into me last night. I kissed Preston, which was a shock in and of itself, but to go so far as to come home with him … what was I thinking? I can only say I wasn't thinking. Not with my brain anyway. I was thinking what it would be like to be set alight by his touch. How he'd make me feel, how he'd taste … I was going on instinct instead of being my usual "think before I act" self.

I wake up in an unfamiliar bed and look across at an empty space next to me. That's odd. It's his house, so why would he leave? It's also Sunday, so I'm sure he's not working. Although he does seem to be a 24/7 workaholic.

Dressing in the same dress I wore last night, I mentally kick myself for having my high heels in my hand, ready for the walk of shame. I'm a little disappointed in myself—this isn't something I normally do—but I need to sneak out of the house and pretend last night never happened.

How am I meant to forget last night though? It was, for want of a more descriptive word, incredible. Preston is intoxicating. He's like a drug—one hit and I'm addicted. The sex was … phenomenal. He certainly knows what he's doing in that department. I lost count of the orgasms he gave me. All I know is my knees went weak and my body went limp, almost like I'd slipped into a coma or something. A sex-induced coma. Is that a thing? I'm sure that's what it was.

Now I'm feeling like another notch on his bedpost. He doesn't actually have a bedpost, but if he did, I can imagine it being pretty marked from where he handcuffs women, takes what he wants and then sends them on their way.

My god, why am I even thinking like this? My thoughts are scattered, and I am going from "he's an incredible lover who is capable of being more caring than I thought possible" to "he treats women like a used tissue". I need to get out of my own head. I should be giving him more credit than that.

As I walk quietly down the hall to the stairway, I'm greeted by nothing but deafening silence. There's no sign of him at all. Where is he? Can I sneak out completely unnoticed? Is he waiting in a room somewhere until he hears the front door close behind me?

Looking at my surroundings, I can see why his office building is so well furnished. He's a man with extremely good taste. There are gorgeous paintings on the walls, a couple of sculptures on end tables … If I had to describe his home in one word, it would be "exquisite". Well, what I've seen of it so far, that is.

I'm tiptoeing around like a teenage girl who doesn't want to wake her parents as she sneaks out to meet a boy. Only, I'm sneaking out away from the boy instead. Why can't I just be an adult and face him? Because I'd blush like an idiot, knowing he knows me intimately now and that we can never go back to how we were before. Because I'd stumble over my words and embarrass myself—and most likely him—in the process. If ever there was a facepalm moment for being an idiot, this would probably be it. When I see Paisley at work tomorrow, she will grill me, and I will blame it all on the whiskey we were drinking like it was water. I'm not normally a lightweight, but I can convince her. I think. Who am I trying to kid here? Myself probably.

I'm at the bottom of the stairs and I hear a sound. I stand completely immobile, trying to figure out where the noise is coming from. It sounds like a coffee machine and I take a deep breath as I smell the beautiful aroma. I almost want to stay. Almost. I could have a coffee with him and make small talk. But I feel too shy, too awkward.

Sucking in a deep breath, I try to pull my scattered thoughts together to make something coherent. I walk towards the front door, but there's a door slightly ajar in the hallway. I want to see more of his home; I'm intrigued by him. He's an enigma and I want to know him better. But at the same time, I don't. I just want to go back to the non-existent relationship we had before last night.

Acting before thinking it through fully, I peek my head around the door. It looks like a home office. There's a huge cherry wood desk taking up the space in front of the window. I push the door open slightly more and I slip inside as quietly as I can. All I can see behind the desk is the back of the chair, but the rest of the room is amazing. There's a massive bookshelf with a book collection. Some of the books look older. Maybe they're first editions—after all, I know he has the money for that kind of thing.

I run my hand down some of the spines, loving the feeling of soft leather beneath my fingers. In my spare time, I love to read. I have a loveseat at home that I snuggle up on with a blanket over my lap, a mug of cocoa and a good book. I am addicted to my Kindle because I can download new releases as soon as they come out, but there's nothing that can beat the feeling of a real book in my hands. The smell of the pages is something I love, although I can't explain why.

Looking around the vast space, I notice artwork on the walls and a beautiful Tiffany lamp on a small table next to a wingback armchair. Maybe that's where Preston likes to sit and read. I can picture him there, looking sexy with tousled hair and dressed in low slung jeans instead of the suits I normally see him in. He'd have a steaming mug of coffee or cocoa on the table, a book in his hands, and he'd be absorbed in the story. I wonder what kind of books he likes to read. No doubt he doesn't read romance stories. I have him down as a fantasy lover, maybe JRR Tolkien or George RR Martin ...

"Morning sunshine."

I jump at the sound of his husky voice. I turn back and see him sitting in the desk chair. He looks handsome in a casual t-shirt. I wonder what he's wearing on the bottom half. Something that clings to his gorgeous ass and strong thighs would be good.

"Morning," I say as I feel a blush creep up my neck and face. The phrase "caught red-handed" springs to mind.

"Can I get you a coffee?" he asks as he stands and walks towards me.

He's wearing indigo jeans, slung low on his hips. Oh, those hips. He's got an incredible physique. Closing my eyes, I picture him naked. The hard planes of his body, his strong biceps, washboard abs, that sexy V that turns women to a puddle of goo; he has it all.

"Coffee?" he asks, shocking me into opening my eyes.

"Umm...," I'm lost for words. Why can't I just say something? Anything! For heaven's sake, Nye, wake the hell up and speak to the guy.

He walks past me, opens the office door and strides out, his back to me. His ass looks great in those jeans. They fit him well. I have a feeling he'd look good in anything. He certainly looks good in nothing, that I know for sure.

Dragging my mind out of the gutter, I follow him out of the office and down the hallway.

His kitchen has to be the most impressive room I've seen in his house. Admittedly I didn't actually get much time to look at his bedroom, but his office was gorgeous. But the kitchen? Wow! The huge floor to ceiling windows let in a lot of natural light and I can see an orangery set off the back of the glass doors.

The top of the kitchen island looks like it's made of granite or something exquisite and expensive. All of the mod cons are chrome and black. They could look out of place in an Edwardian home, but he's had everything made so that it fits well. It's sympathetic to the home around it.

Preston's back is towards me as he fiddles with the coffee machine. I can't tell what kind it is, but I'm sure it's expensive. He doesn't seem the type to have something like my Nespresso. He's more the type to have something imported that only uses a certain type of coffee bean. Why am I thinking about coffee? I'm trying not to think how his muscles look as he moves. His back is broad and strong and I'm wondering whether it bears the marks of my nails digging into it last night.

"How do you take it?" he asks, making me jump.

"White with sweetener rather than sugar, if you have any, please."

He reaches into a cupboard and his t-shirt lifts, showing me his sun-kissed skin underneath. I find myself wanting to reach out and touch him, maybe lick a trail along the exposed skin … I really need to get a grip.

He turns to face me and coughs, and I look up to meet his chocolate gaze. His eyes look more amber in this light. They are nothing short of magnificent, just like the rest of him.

Pulling out a stool at the kitchen island, he gestures for me to sit. I'm sure he caught me staring, but he's gentlemanly enough not to mention it.

We sit next to each other and his leg touches mine. His covered in denim, mine still exposed because of the length of the dress. The mere touch of him feels like a jolt of electricity through my entire body. The hairs at the nape of my neck stand on end and my skin is hyper-sensitive to his touch. Suddenly I want to be back in his bed, underneath him, on top of him … any way I can get him.

I am squeezing my legs together to try and quell the sensation stirring down there. I'm not sure that just once was enough with him. But I'm also not sure of where we go from here. We hooked up. It doesn't automatically equal two point four children, a dog, a house with a white picket fence. Though I'd be lying if I said that outcome wouldn't appeal to me. I want to settle down with someone and start a family one day. It's just, can I really do that with someone like Preston? He has everything I don't. Money for starters. He's running his family business and building his empire, whilst I run a clothing store. Okay, technically I own my own boutique, but that doesn't mean I earn a lot of money. A lot of my profits are plowed back into the business, that's just the way it goes. I only keep back enough to pay Paisley a salary and of course pay my own bills.

He also has this amazing house and whilst I own my own house, it's nowhere near as grand as this place.

What could I honestly offer this guy that he doesn't have? Why am I even thinking this way in the first place? We hooked up. It's not like he's going to fall head over heels in love with me, no matter how mind-blowing the sex was.

"Penny for them?" Preston says, bringing me back to the here and now.

"Sorry, I was in a world of my own."

I laugh and try to shake off the thoughts racing through my mind.

"What are your plans for today?" he asks as he takes a large gulp of his coffee.

"Nothing really. Sunday is the only day the store is closed. Paisley and I sometimes get together and go for lunch over in Blue Ridge. But we haven't planned to today."

"Would you like to do something together?"

Color me surprised. I didn't think he'd want to spend more time with me.

"What were you thinking?"

"I don't know. Maybe we could go for lunch somewhere. Or I could cook if I popped out to pick a few things up."

The sound of staying here for lunch is appealing. It might give me some more insight into the mystery that is Preston Fitzgerald. So much for the walk of shame.

"I think I'd need to go home and change."

"Sure thing, I can drop you home."

He flashes me that Hollywood smile and I'm glad I'm already sitting down because it makes me weak in the knees.

"I could shower and change, then drive back here."

"Sounds like a plan. Shall we get going?"

He stands up and I can't help but drink in the sight of him. He really is otherworldly. Possibly the most handsome man I have ever met.

***

I feel better after a hot shower. More like myself. Less like a hormonal teenager wanting to climb that man like a tree.

Leaving my hair down to dry naturally, I look in my wardrobe to try and choose an outfit. I'm not sure what to wear. Do I dress for comfort or do I wear something that goes with the only pair of Louboutins I actually own?

Will Preston be likely to wear a suit? Surely not for Sunday lunch. Does he do casual clothes? Well, he must do because he was in jeans and a t-shirt earlier, but that was probably a rarity and only because he was inside his own home. I remember last night he told me something about not having many casual clothes. He said he normally wears a shirt and trousers. That's his version of casual.

I spot a cashmere sweater that I'd all but forgotten I own, pull it out and inspect it. Emerald green, V-neck but nothing low or slutty. I can pair it with my butt-hugging jeans—as Paisley likes to call them—and a pair of comfy boots. I almost want to wear my cowboy boots to show him that I really own a pair, but I go for my black, knee-length soft leather boots instead.

I pull my outfit together, lay it out on my bed and let the towel drop from around me. I pull on my favorite matching bra and panties. Lacy and sexy, probably the most expensive set I own. You pay good money for comfort and style. Or at least I do.

I slip into my favorite black jeans, zip them up and grab my sweater. Once I'm fully dressed, I sit in front of my vanity and apply minimal makeup. I don't like to be too heavy-handed and I have a feeling Preston prefers natural-looking women.

I smile to myself as I make my way to my car. Today has the potential to be a good day.

Chapter Six

Preston

I don't know what came over me, inviting Nye for lunch. I don't offer to cook for anyone. I mean, I can cook—I'm a single man who has to take care of himself, after all—but I don't cook for other people, especially not women that I slept with the night before.

I also don't do nervous. But here I am with sweaty palms, wondering what to wear. Ninety-nine percent of the time, I'm in a shirt and smart trousers, but this morning, she saw me in jeans and a t-shirt. She didn't seem to mind that I was dressed so casually. Why am I standing here looking in my wardrobe caring what Nye thinks? I'm usually pretty vain about my appearance anyway—I like to know I look good—but I'm being extra vain today. I want her to look at me and crave me the way she did last night.

Oh, last night. To say it was mind-blowing is an understatement. The sex was incredible. Her body reacted to my every movement; every little touch elicited gasps from her gorgeous lips. And oh, those lips. Her kisses were addictive, her lips trailing across my abs, down to the V that women go gaga over, then she took my throbbing cock in her mouth and I almost blew my load there and then. Schoolboy error well avoided, thank god.

I grab a pair of dark blue ripped jeans—yes, they are designer—and a black V-neck t-shirt. Once I'm dressed, I use some of my favorite cologne, Valentino V. I love the notes of sandalwood, cedar and musk. There's something inherently manly about this particular scent. I find myself hoping Nye will like it.

Part of me wants to be a gentleman and go and pick her up for lunch, but the other part of me says it's easier if she comes in her own car, just in case she decides to leave in a hurry—perhaps regretting what happened between us last night. I have no such regrets myself, but she might see me in a different light the morning—okay technically afternoon—after the night before.

Last night was … amazing, incredible, intoxicating … more than I ever expected it to be. I felt like I might spontaneously combust just from seeing her completely naked—a sight now permanently etched into my mind. From feeling the touch of her silky skin beneath my hands. From looking into her eyes and seeing the hunger in them. Why did she have to feel like heaven on earth? How did she get under my skin so quickly, or in fact, at all?

I hear the intercom, so I hurry to the monitor and double-check it's her car before opening the gates.

I guess this house could seem imposing at first. Nye probably thinks I'm a bit odd for having such security in a small town like Snowflake, but with the reputation my grandfather built, there are some people that would sooner see me on my knees with nothing but the clothes on my back, much less a house and car like mine. My grandfather was a ruthless bastard and I often find myself wondering whether he had a heart or just an empty chest cavity. I always thought it was the latter.

I open the front door and see her park her car next to mine. I walk out and open her door for her.

"And here was me thinking chivalry was dead," she says with a smile as she stands and takes the hand I'm holding out.

"I'm nothing if not the perfect gentleman," I reply with a smirk.

I close her car door and walk her to the porch. She stops and looks up at the house.

"I'd be happy to give you the grand tour."

"I'd like that."

A sheepish grin form on her pretty little lips, which, I notice, are painted a soft pink today.

"Great, shall we have lunch first?"

"That would be great, yeah. What are we having?"

"Oh shit, I forgot to ask. You aren't vegetarian, are you?"

"I'm guessing I wouldn't be having much for lunch if I was, am I right?"

Now it's my turn to look a little sheepish as I lead her into the house.

"Well, you could still eat the vegetables, and you could have second helpings…" I offer with a laugh.

"It's okay, I'm not vegetarian. You're safe. So, what's on the menu?"

"I'm planning on grilling a spatchcock chicken and combining it with jersey royal potatoes cooked in wild garlic, with savoy cabbage, parsnips and carrots. That's if you have no objections? I can do other vegetables if you prefer?"

I had it all planned out in my head, but now Nye is here, and I am second-guessing myself. I love to cook, and I find I have a good sense of what goes together, but I should have asked before she left if she had any preferences or allergies or was, in fact, vegetarian.

"That sounds delicious."

Her stomach rumbles and I laugh.

I walk her through to the kitchen and pull out a stool at the island for her opposite where I am prepping the vegetables. I pick up my peeler and begin on the carrots.

"Your home really is beautiful, well, what I've seen of it. This kitchen is incredible. I'd be in heaven with a kitchen like this. I love to cook, and I have cooker envy right now. That's a real thing, you know. Your range cooker is something I'd love to fit in my kitchen, but it's too small and poky for something that size."

Her rambling is cute. She's actually very cute indeed. No, she's more than that, she's striking. Today she's in an emerald sweater—which to my eye looks like it's made from cashmere—which highlights her eye color. Her black jeans accentuate what a great ass she has—I couldn't help but watch as she took a seat—and her boots look comfy but also sexy. With minimal makeup, she looks naturally beautiful. Her lips are a soft pink and I could be wrong but it looks like gloss rather than lipstick. She also smells divine: a combination of her shampoo which smells like apples, and a perfume I can't name.

"Cooker envy is a real thing?" I ask in as serious a tone as I can muster when I'm dying to full-on belly laugh at her remark.

"It is. I've been wishing I had a bigger kitchen for so long. I want to be able to fit a range in there, a sleek black one like yours. I could bake until my heart was content."

She's a baker? I can just picture her in an apron, with flour everywhere. Sexy.

"Watch what you're doing, you'll slice through your finger," she says, making me look down to my hand.

"Shit!"

I grab my finger and rush to put it under the cold tap.

"Do you have a first aid kit?"

"Umm … somewhere."

I wrap a tea towel around my hand and rush to open cupboards, trying to locate the small kit. Once I have it in hand, Nye takes it from me and ushers me to sit on the stool she's vacated. Damn my mind for wandering to what she'd look like wearing nothing but an apron and flour in her hair.

"Here, let me," she says as she unwraps the hastily wrapped tea towel.

Taking my injured hand in hers, she looks at the cut. Thankfully, it isn't too large, nor does it look too deep.

"I don't think you'll need proper stitches, these should do the trick."

She lifts a pack of butterfly stitches—or Steri-Strips, whatever you want to call them.

"I'm such an idiot. Here's me saying I'll be doing spatchcock chicken when I can't even peel a carrot."

"I tell you what, I'll take over the peeling, and how about we just roast the chicken instead?"

"I don't expect you to help me cook, you're a guest."

"Like I said, I like to cook. I don't mind peeling whilst you prepare the chicken."

I look at my hand and decide to forego my usual pride.

"Thank you."

Offering me a small smile, Nye continues to tend to my injured finger. As soon as it's sorted, she tidies away the first aid kit and deposits the rubbish in the bin. Next, she pulls an apron from the hook and picks up the peeler.

I didn't intend for her to have to help me, but I can't deny she looks right at home in my kitchen.

As spatchcocking involves a knife and me deboning the chicken, I decide Nye was right, I'm just going to roast it instead.

I go about retrieving the chicken from the fridge and a roasting tin from the cupboard as Nye happily peels and hums a familiar tune.

Then I walk over to my Bose soundbar, select the tune and turn the volume up a little. "Country Girl" plays and Nye turns to me with a smile on her face.

Holding my hands up, I look at her and laugh.

"Yes, I own this album. I said you looked like a country girl, but I didn't say I liked or disliked country, did I?"

"I guess not," she laughs. "I just didn't have you down as owning a Luke Bryan album. I know you said your taste is eclectic, but…"

"I'll let you into a secret—I think he has a great voice. I've seen him live too."

"That makes two of us."

***

After bonding over our love of live music, Nye hooks her phone up to the soundbar and selects a track.

She holds out her hand towards me and I envelop her tiny palm in mine. It feels like it was made to fit perfectly. She takes my other hand and places it on her hip and it takes me a moment to realize that she's asking me to dance.

We dance around my kitchen without a care in the world. Nye's expression is one of happiness and maybe a touch of silliness as we dance around to Bruno Mars's "Locked Out of Heaven". It's a good job this room is a decent size, good enough to dance in. It's not my normal choice of song to dance to, but Nye could probably make me do just about anything. All she'd have to do is flutter those long dark eyelashes at me and I'd give her whatever she asked.

After the song ends, Nye checks on the vegetables while I watch her looking at home in my kitchen.

Her hair falls over her shoulders in soft curls that linger close to her voluptuous breasts. The sweater she's wearing doesn't cling to her curves, but it does enhance them.

As if she knows I'm looking at her, her eyes lift to meet mine and her lips curve in a heart-stopping smile.

I decide to set the small table in the orangery. It seems less formal than setting up the large oak table in the dining room.

With the table set for two, I set about finding a nice bottle of white wine and some filtered water.

"I don't drink when I'm driving," Nye remarks.

"I'm sorry, I should have asked, I wasn't thinking. You could always get a cab home, or the other option is the filtered water I just put on the table. In fact, I'll drink water too."

"Don't be silly, you're in your own home, of course, you can drink."

***

After lunch, the two of us move into the lounge. She's sitting with her feet curled under her in my favorite armchair. She looks relaxed and happy, which looks good on her. It's been so long since I felt this comfortable around someone. What is it about this woman in particular that makes you want to let down your walls and let her in?

I won't lie, I would love for her to stay again tonight, to give her a repeat performance of last night. But I don't want to rush. Too much too soon and all that.

All too soon, I see Nye check her watch. She notices me watching her.

"I'm sorry, I'll have to get going soon. I'm opening up in the morning."

"No worries. I have work to do myself in the morning. There's no rest for the wicked."

"You should be good then, perhaps you'd get a break once in a while."

"Oh, ha ha, very funny. I can be a very good boy, or I can be very naughty. It depends on my mood and the company I'm keeping."

She giggles, and I don't think I've ever heard a sweeter sound.

We spend another hour talking before I see her to the door.

I lean down to kiss her on the cheek, but she turns her head at the same time and I end up kissing her on the lips. She gasps in shock before slipping her arms up around my neck, pulling me closer and deepening the kiss at the same time.

My heart beats erratically as I slip an arm around her waist and the other hand up into her hair. Pulling her hair back gently, I expose her throat and begin to place soft kisses along her jaw. Moving my way down to the hollow of her throat, I hear her panting, and see her chest heaving with each breath she takes.

She pulls back from me, and I watch as she draws a couple of deep breaths to regain her composure.

"Goodnight Preston."

"Goodnight Aneurin."

"How many times must I tell you, it's Nye."

I smirk at her and shrug my shoulders.

"My apologies. It's a beautiful name for a beautiful lady, but if you insist, goodnight Nye."

Chapter Seven

Nye

It's been two days since I saw Preston. Part of me wants to drop him a text and see how he is, but as I haven't heard from him, I refuse to be the one to do the chasing.

Of course, when I got back to work yesterday, Paisley pressed me for all the juicy details. A lady doesn't kiss and tell, but I told her we had a good time and he seems like a good guy once you get past all his extravagance. She knows about the lunch date, but I couldn't bring myself to tell her I'd gone home with him the night before. It's not like I'm embarrassed, but I don't want her thinking I throw myself at the first man who comes along. I know she's known me for a long time, but nonetheless, I don't want to tarnish her opinion of me.

The store has been busy today, what with the Christmas sale event we have going on. I'm glad to have the room for more stock, but I detest stocktaking. I'd hoped I could rope Paisley into helping me, but Jack whisked her away for a date this evening. So, here I am, sitting in the stockroom going cross-eyed as I try to do it all alone. Truth be told, I'm exhausted, but I need to go to the warehouse in Blue Ridge for more stock if I'm to have anything to sell in the store in the next few days.

After more hours than I care to count, I'm finally on my way to Mistletoe & Wine for a well-deserved glass of wine.

Walking in, I see Preston sat at the bar. He's talking to some blonde who seems more his type—aesthetically speaking—than me. I don't know whether to feel hurt or not. It could well be something innocent, or he could be moving on to the next notch on his bedpost already. I can't tell from this distance.

I sit in a booth by the window, hoping not to attract his attention. Kacey, who works the bar, sees me and wanders over with a glass of my favorite wine in her hand. I almost ask her if she knows who Preston is talking to, considering the bar staff get to overhear a lot of goings on, but I bite my tongue.

As I sit on my own, I wonder who the woman is. She's not a local, otherwise I'd know her. Snowflake is a place where everyone pretty much knows everyone else. She's dressed to impress, by the looks of it. She's wearing a pretty, purple dress that falls just short of her knee; her long, blonde hair is straight and falls to the middle of her back. I can't see her face from my position, but she's probably all made up, looking like an airbrushed model. Why do I even care? I really don't know. Maybe it's just because I was in his bed two nights ago and didn't think I'd be replaced so soon. But who am I fooling? After all, nobody is irreplaceable.

Kacey comes to join me for a drink on her break and we make small talk about the upcoming tree-lighting and other Christmas festivities going on around the town. My mind isn't really on the conversation as I watch the blonde twirling her hair, brushing her thigh against Preston's … I excuse myself from Kacey's company and head to the ladies' room.

Splashing a little cold water on my face, I look at my reflection in the mirror. Is it true that women can't distinguish sex from feelings? Is it that after only one night and Sunday lunch the following day, I was beginning to see Preston through different eyes than when he first came to town? I thought he actually liked me, maybe wanted to see where it might lead between us. How stupid. Somebody from a background like his, from a family with money, wouldn't look at me as more than a bit of fun. After all, they only have lasting relationships with people of their own caliber—other people with money—surely?! I was a fool to think he might have seen us differently.

With my mind made up to forget Preston and move on, I walk out of the room with my head held high.

As I walk past the bar back to my seat, Preston's voice stops me in my tracks.

"Aneurin."

I turn on my heel to face him. His face lights up with his signature smile.

"Good evening, Preston."

I'm trying to remain as impassive as possible.

"Good evening. Are you well?"

"Yes, thank you. Are you?" I reply, trying to remain polite.

"Yes, thank you. May I introduce you to Cordelia."

She looks at me and I see she's the epitome of an airbrushed model straight out of Vogue.

"Cordelia, this is Nye. Nye, meet Cordelia."

"It's a pleasure to meet you, Cordelia."

I extend my hand for her to shake and, as she does the same, I see her highly manicured nails and her creamy soft skin.

"The pleasure is all mine," she says in a cordial enough tone, but I see her eyes flare at me.

Assuming I'm imagining the small degree of animosity, I smile widely at her, trying to show I mean no harm to whatever she has going on with Preston.

She looks at me with venom in her glare. Why does she have a problem with me when she doesn't know me from Eve? There must be more to her and Preston than I had assumed. As I haven't seen her around before, I can only come to the conclusion that they know each other from before he moved here. Maybe they have had a long-distance relationship and what he and I had was because he was pining for her and he just used me because I was here and more than willing to go home with him that night.

Whatever is happening, I have no intention of sticking around to see just how venomous Cordelia can be. They say first impressions are everything and if that's true, then I can see no future in which this woman could come to like me, nor I her.

"If you don't mind, Preston, I am waiting on a friend. I must go and see if she's arrived."

I turn to walk back to my booth with a feeling of unshed tears stinging my eyes. I feel so utterly dejected and completely stupid. How did I assume I was good enough for someone like him when he belongs with the Cordelias of the world?

"Have a good night," he calls as I walk away.

Back at my booth, I tap out a text to my friend Trina, asking if she fancies a quick drink. I haven't seen her in a while and it would be good to catch up. Of course, I wouldn't have necessarily met up with her tonight if it wasn't for Preston. But I did say I was meeting a friend and rather than look a fool, or just go home, I wait for her reply, while drinking a glass of wine Kacey has left on the table for me.

Twenty minutes later, I see Trina walk through the door and I smile my first genuine smile of the evening.

***

An hour of gossiping with Trina makes me feel more like myself. I feel relaxed and less stressed than I did when I first walked into the bar.

I'm in the ladies' room, reapplying my lipstick in the mirror, when who should walk in but Cordelia. I flick my gaze over to her and she looks even more beautiful in the better lighting. She catches me looking at her and huffs haughtily before walking into a stall and slamming the door shut.

I drag my fingers through my hair and wish I hadn't come straight from work. I'm not dressed anywhere near as nicely as her. Even my finest clothes aren't as expensive as the dress she's wearing, or the Jimmy Choos on her feet. I do own one pair of red Louboutins that were a gift a lifetime ago from my father, but my clothes aren't designer, and the perfume I wear isn't anything extravagant. I find myself comparing the two of us when no comparisons should be made. There are no parallels to be drawn. We are as diametrically opposed as two people could be. I'd thought the same about Preston and me before, then I'd lost sight of it for a while. Cordelia reminds me just how different we truly are.

For the second time this evening, I let out a long sigh and wish things were different. But they aren't, so I just have to make the best of the situation. I'll sweep it under the rug and forget Preston and I ever happened. It was, after all, only one night and day spent in each other's company. Yes, he kissed me goodbye on the Sunday like he'd like a repeat performance in the future…or at least I thought he had. My imagination must know no bounds. I would hazard a guess that maybe there'd have been a repeat performance if Cordelia hadn't turned up in Snowflake, but I'd say she was always bound to turn up at some point.

Perhaps it's better to know now. Sure, I'm hurting in the short-term, but that's better than letting it go any further between us and then getting hurt more. I guess that's all the positive I can take from this situation.

Cordelia exits the stall behind me and huffs as she walks to the sink to wash her hands. I don't even know why I'm still standing here at this point, but now I'm rooted to the spot. I'm determined not to let her break me—externally at least.

"You do know he can't be with you, don't you?" she asks, her brusque tone pulling me up short.

"Who?"

"You know full well who. He's rich—filthy rich really—and he could never lower himself to being with someone who doesn't come from money and good breeding."

"What an awful thing to say. You know nothing about me. My father is actually very rich himself, my mother too. And they are wonderful people, there is nothing wrong with my breeding," I respond, air-quoting the word breeding.

"Yet you dress like some … street urchin," she spits with disgust lacing her tone.

"How dare you."

Before I have time to think through my actions, I slap her hard across that smug face of hers.

Reeling from my slap, she totters back on her Jimmy Choos and comes to rest against the wall.

"What the…" she trails off as she looks at herself in the mirror.

There's a red handprint on her face. It might be faint, but it's there all the same. She looks at herself, shock crossing her features. I'm starting to think nobody has ever stood up to her before. Well, she might be used to getting her way wherever it is she comes from, but not here, not with me.

"You little bitch," she seethes.

"You don't know me, nor what I am capable of. Stay out of my way and I'll stay out of yours … and your precious Preston's."

She raises her hand as if to hit me back, but when you don't want an enemy to know what you're about to do, you shouldn't be so obvious about it. I sidestep her easily and her hand sails through the air, no connection made.

"Like I said, stay out of my way and I'll repay the favor."

With that, I turn and leave the room. I take a deep breath as I draw my shoulders back and hold my head high once more, bracing myself to pass Preston on my way back to Trina.

Reaching my booth unscathed, I tell Trina I'm tired and should really call it a night. My hands are shaking with the aftermath of losing my temper, so I hold them behind my back where she can't see.

We bid each other goodnight and I grab my coat and walk out of the pub, not looking at Preston until I am safe in the shadow of the night. I allow myself a brief glimpse at him before turning my back to him and leaving.

***

Safe behind the walls of my own home, I allow myself to crumple in a heap and cry. Why I'm even crying, I'm not entirely sure. It could be the shock of having slapped someone for the first time since high school—where I only did it once in defense of myself when I was being bullied for having braces—or maybe it's because of the things she said about my breeding, my not being suited for a man such a Preston Fitzgerald. Maybe it's because I spent the night with him and thought I could come to have feelings for him in the future if I wasn't careful. Perhaps I'm mourning that fantasy future … Perhaps it's a mixture of everything.

Once I've cried until I can cry no more, I head to my room and grab a towel. In my en-suite, I turn the shower temperature to hot before stripping and stepping in.

The heat feels good on my weary, aching bones. I slide to the floor and sit under the spray of water, letting it beat down on me and wash away my tears as I let my head fall back against the wall.

After sitting in the shower until my skin resembles a bowl of prunes, I get out and dry myself off. I slip into my pajamas and cocoon myself in the blankets, hoping to drift off into a dreamless sleep.

Chapter Eight

Nye

It's been a week since the incident and I haven't seen Preston once. Thankfully, I haven't seen Cordelia either, and I haven't stepped foot inside the pub since, just in case they were in there.

Paisley knows all about what happened and swore she'd try and find out from Jack who this Cordelia woman is and what gave her the right to—and I quote—*have such a stick up her ass.* I told her not to ask on my behalf, I'd rather forget it and forget them. Plus, things seem to be going really well between her and Jack, I wouldn't want to be the cause of any problems.

They actually seem to be the perfect match. All lovey-dovey and puke-inducing affection. I'm happy for my best friend, but sad for myself. I wish I had what she does. I wish Preston and I had been given the chance to see if we could have a future.

Paisley has a constant smile on her face and whenever her phone chimes with a text, she radiates happiness. I'm glad Jack can make her feel like that. I, however, haven't received a single text from Preston, nor have I texted him. I'm left to assume Cordelia told him what I did and now he's avoiding me at all costs. That's fine by me, and the Christmas trade in the store has kept my mind occupied. It's only when I'm alone at home on an evening that I allow myself to even think of his name. Although I wish I could erase him completely.

I seem to have lost weight and I don't know whether to blame it on all the rushing about I've been doing at work and occasionally forgetting to eat lunch, or whether it's due to stress.

Refusing myself to wallow any longer, I look at myself in the bathroom mirror and steel myself against the onslaught of feelings.

My feelings are useless. Preston and I, well, it's just a moot point. No point in dwelling.

I walk into the lounge, grab my box of Christmas decorations. I set my iPod to play festive songs, my favorite album, *On This Winter's Night.*

With a glass of red wine in my hand, I set about hanging decorations—garlands across my inglenook fireplace and pine cones along the top of the mantelpiece. I admire my handiwork before moving onto the rest of the room.

My tree looks amazing, even if I do say so myself. I have a mixture of decorations on there, some old and some new. Growing up, we had traditional decorations to hang, but when my parents divorced, I asked if I could keep the box so that I could keep the tradition going. Of course, Evelyn, or should I call her "mother", was insistent that she got to keep some too, so we ended up splitting them three ways between me and my parents.

Admiring my creativity, I pour myself another glass of wine. I settle down on the couch, pick up a book—*A Winter's Tale* by Carrie Elks—and pull my feet up underneath me to read for a while. I love Christmas stories pretty much any time of the year—I am a bit like a child who truly loves the magic of Christmas—but now is the perfect time to read them, with only three weeks to go until Christmas Day.

My phone chimes with a text:

Paisley: Jack says things aren't as they seem with Cordelia, but he won't expand on how. Want me to try and dig some more?

I told her I didn't want her to risk things between her and Jack just to check things out for me. I type out a quick response, wanting to get back to my book, to escape reality for a while.

Nye: I told you, didn't I? I said don't ask him anything. Don't ask him anything else, please. It wasn't meant to be with me and Preston. There's no insta-love for me like the romance books I read.

I see the three dots bouncing, meaning she's replying.

Paisley: Nye, you mean the world to me and I want more than anything to see you happy. Maybe you don't believe in "insta-love", but you do believe in love. Don't let this experience put you off men. Don't let it put you off, Preston. Seriously girl, you fight for those who mean something for you!

But does he mean something to me? I thought he *could*, but that doesn't mean he does. Yet.

Nye: Don't worry about me, Pais, I'm fine. I promise.

Paisley: Pfft! Where's my feisty best friend gone? Have you seen her? I miss her.

Nye: You don't call slapping Cordelia "feisty"?

Paisley: You know what I mean. My best friend is a confident, sexy woman who won't stop at anything to get her man.

I let out a long sigh and take a deep gulp of my wine before replying.

Nye: Please, Paisley. Please, just let it drop. I'm good, I swear.

Paisley: Okay. I'll let it drop. For now.

I sigh in resignation, knowing this won't be the last I hear of it.

I walk to the kitchen and pour myself another glass of wine. As I head back to the lounge, I hear my phone ring. Assuming it's Paisley, I pick it up and answer without checking who it is.

"Hello Aneurin," a familiar voice says.

My skin breaks out in goosebumps and I feel the hairs on the back of my neck rise. I mentally kick myself for not checking the caller ID and sending him to voicemail.

"Hello Preston."

My tone is flat. I am trying to be cordial, but I'll probably fail. I'm far too emotional for that.

"Can we talk?" he asks quietly.

We haven't spoken for a week and now he wants to talk all of a sudden?!

"Is it business or pleasure?"

"What?"

"This phone call, is it for business or pleasure?"

"Well…"

Preston is never normally at a loss for words.

"I'm kind of busy here, Preston, so if it's for anything other than business, I don't have time for idle chitchat."

My tone is harsher than I would have liked, but I can already feel tears stinging my eyes. I can't stay on the phone to him, it's going to break my resolve.

"I just wanted to say I'm sorry for not calling sooner."

I don't know what he wants me to say.

"I agree, you could have called me sooner. I don't normally sleep with a guy and then not hear from him for a week. Especially having spent the whole day together on the Sunday, thinking maybe it was the start of something, when all along you had another woman in the wings."

Okay, so I kind of blurted that out.

"Another woman? Are we at crossed wires, here, Aneurin?"

"No, there's nothing crossed. I know about her. Well, not much, but I know she exists. Look, I'm sorry Preston, but I really have a lot to do."

I hang up the phone before he can reply.

Feeling hollow and dejected, I drain my glass and decide on an early night.

Pulling my pajamas on, I hear my phone buzzing, having set it to silent after hanging up. I can't even be bothered to check if it's Preston or Paisley. I don't want to speak to anyone right now. I just want to go to sleep and wake up to a new start tomorrow.

Chapter Nine

Preston

I don't know what Aneurin meant about another woman waiting in the wings. I don't know how she came to that conclusion. I know I haven't spoken to her for a while, although I admit that until she told me, I didn't realize it had been so long.

Work has kept me extremely busy this week. I've had so much to do and so little time. Add to that the fact that my bloody ex turned up on my doorstep. I couldn't believe it when I saw her.

Cordelia has worked for my grandfather's company since the days when he ran it. That's how we met. She was at work in the office and I was called in by my grandfather to a meeting in the boardroom. I didn't really work for him at the time—I did some odd work on occasion—but I went in for meetings as and when he called me. He commanded my attendance and I didn't want to piss him off. He was an angry man most of the time, so he was even worse when you went against his wishes.

That day, Cordelia had been in the meeting, transcribing the notes. She had long blonde hair, legs that went on for miles and baby blue eyes. She was the exact type I normally went for. Of course, my grandfather approved. It turned out he'd only called me into the office that day because he wanted us to meet. He wasn't a matchmaker, but he thought she was worthy of someone of the Fitzgerald name. I didn't find that out until we'd been dating for three months.

We were never meant to be, and I didn't do relationships. I wasn't up for more than a bit of fun and Cordelia didn't seem to want anything serious either. It seemed a good way of keeping my grandfather off my case. Until the day she told me she was pregnant.

I was dumbfounded. I'd made sure she was on the pill before we ever slept together, and she swore she didn't want anything serious to tie her down. Plus, she said she wasn't sure she ever wanted kids, let alone while she was so young.

When my grandfather found out, he was over the moon. I'd have an heir for the family business. He only ever cared about carrying on the bloodline. I hadn't intended to tell him so soon, but Cordelia had told her mother who also worked for the company and she'd let it slip to him.

Two months passed, and Cordelia was a nightmare to be around. She kept trying to talk about getting married. I don't know what happened to the woman who didn't want something serious. I wasn't one hundred percent sure she hadn't gotten pregnant just to trap me, which sounded stupid in my head, but things now felt weird with her.

The day for her three-month scan came and we went along to the hospital. The sonographer was silent as she scanned Cordelia's mostly flat stomach. She wasn't even showing yet, which was good because we didn't want it getting out at work until after the first scan.

Then came the worst news we could have asked for. The sonographer had gone to get somebody else to come in and look—a second opinion I guess. Then she told us that she was sorry, but there was no baby. We must have lost our baby in utero. Cordelia broke down. She wept for our baby and I held her as she kept asking the same thing. Why did it happen to us? What had she done wrong?

The truth was, she hadn't done anything wrong. It just wasn't meant to be. We returned to my home that afternoon and I held her as she cried and rocked back and forth on the bed. She cried herself to sleep and I lay there, holding her as she slept. I couldn't figure out why it had happened because there was no real reason. I always liked to be in control and know what happened, when, where, why and how. But this was something I was never going to have a concrete answer to.

The following day, after having a little time for it to sink in, Cordelia had an appointment scheduled in hospital. She didn't want me with her and, though I protested, I ended up relenting when she begged me, saying it was something she needed to do alone. It was heartbreaking. Our baby would be gone without a trace after the procedure, almost like he or she had never existed.

A month afterward, Cordelia and I went our separate ways. It was an amicable split, but she said she couldn't see me every day and know that our baby had died. She kept working for the company, but from another office. She'd put in for the transfer and just told my grandfather it was because we were no longer an item.

Until now, I haven't seen her in nearly six years. We've had no reason to see each other or to keep in touch. It was a shock to me when she turned up at the office. I wanted to turn her away but couldn't bring myself to do it. What she wanted was anyone's guess, but I owed it to her to hear her out.

Turns out she's pregnant again. This time, she's four months gone and so she's hoping she can carry it to term. She thought it would be better to come and tell me in person. I honestly don't care. It's not like I was ever in love with her in the first place. The baby meant something to me, but she didn't. I'm ashamed to admit that, but it's the truth.

She thought that it would be better coming to tell me in person rather than me finding out through the company grapevine. I respect her for that, but I still didn't really need to know. If I'd found out any other way, I still wouldn't have cared.

Shit! Now that I think about it, Nye saw Cordelia and I together in Mistletoe & Wine. She must have put two and two together and got five.

I reach for my phone to call her, but my call goes unanswered. I don't want to leave her a voicemail, and a text is too impersonal. What do I do now? I can't just turn up on her doorstep, but I can't leave it unsaid either. She needs to know it's her I am interested in, and that Cordelia means absolutely nothing to me.

I pull up Google on my phone and find the number for the local florist. First thing in the morning, I am going to have a big bouquet delivered to her at work. I don't know her favorite flower, in fact, I know nothing about flowers, but I'll ask the florist for only the prettiest, most fragrant blooms.

I'll also go and see her tomorrow. I want to make it right in person. I want her to know that I am interested in seeing where it goes between us if she's willing to give me the chance.

Pouring myself a decent measure of Macallan, I look at the time and decide to get an early night.

I walk into my en-suite, strip off and set the shower to hot. I put a towel on the heated towel rail then step under the spray. I stand still and let the water wash over me. It's been a tough week at work and I've had no time to see Nye, so the tension knotting my shoulders is to be expected. I don't have an excuse for not calling her or even dropping her a text, only that it's been a really full-on week from hell. I know it only takes a few seconds to tap out a text, but I don't want to only be sparing her a few seconds, I want her to have my undivided attention.

Yes, okay, I've been an idiot. It's to my own detriment. But I'm going to make it up to her if she lets me.

***

I pour myself a glass of orange juice and ring the florist. After discussing the kind of bouquet I want to send, they agree to deliver a bouquet of purple and white calla lilies to *Style in Snowflake* for Nye. I ask the lady to write a message on the card for me. I really don't know what to say, I can't explain things in a few lines on a card. But nevertheless, I ask her to put:

Nye,

I'm sorry I've been so busy and a complete and utter ass. I won't placate you with lame excuses, but please, allow me the chance to try and make it up to you face-to-face.

Preston xx

I've got a few things to deal with at work first thing this morning, so I can't go straight to the store to see her. The florist says they'll make the delivery at ten this morning, so I'm hoping to be done at work by eleven-thirty so that I can be with her for noon and ask her to join me for lunch.

Getting into my car, I take a deep breath, hoping to resolve this situation with Nye. Now I'm stressed not only because of work, but also because I've been an ass and haven't factored in how Nye will be feeling. I'm not used to caring how women feel, but then I'm not used to wanting more with a woman than a little bit of fun. Now, however, my heart pangs with guilt at the thought that she could possibly think I used her. What did she say? I'd slept with her and then not contacted her for a week? That's something the old Preston would have done, but I'm not him anymore. It's not so much that Nye has tamed me, it's not that cliché. It's more that I'm of an age where settling down doesn't frighten me so much anymore. Add in the fact that Nye is not the hook-up kind of girl—she's a woman I can see having more with. For the first time in my life, I can look to my future and see the face of a woman by my side. I've said it before and I'll say it again: she's in my veins. I don't know how to get her out and I don't think I really want to.

***

Work has been non-stop this morning. I'm rattled, and my nerves are frayed. Nye has been at the back of my thoughts in everything I've been doing. Her reaction to me turning up has been bothering me. I'm not sure whether she'll hear me out or whether she'll slam the door in my face.

I can see how she might think Cordelia and I are together, having seen us at the bar. Plus, trying to think like she might, I've realized that she might be angry that I've made time this week to see Cordelia but not her. But it isn't like that. I had to make time for Cordelia because she traveled all this way to see me. She dropped in unannounced and I couldn't really turn her away. I'm hoping Nye is the understanding woman I believe her to be.

It's eleven thirty-five before I get to leave the office. I get in my car and press the button to put the roof down. As I drive in the direction of the store, I begin to feel nervous.

I park the car across the street, so she doesn't see me coming and run a mile.

Looking in through the front window of the store, I don't see Nye and my heart beats hard against my ribs. What if she hasn't come to work today? I see my flowers on the counter, but Paisley could have easily signed for them.

I take a deep breath in, open the door and curse the little bell that signals my arrival. Paisley comes out from the back room and smiles as she sees me.

"Good morning, Paisley." I greet her in a calm voice that belays my inner turmoil.

"Good morning. Nye is out the back. She said she doesn't want to see you. I'm sorry Preston."

My heart falls to my stomach. I had hoped she'd at least be willing to hear me out.

"Would you tell her I'm here? Please, Paisley, I'm here to beg for forgiveness. I'm on my knees here, please?"

Paisley must take pity on me as she goes to the back room without another word.

When she comes back out, her face says it all. Nye doesn't want to know. I feel crushed.

"Thanks for trying, Paisley. Could you tell her that I am sorry? I wish I had the chance to explain."

"I'll tell her, but I'm not sure how much good it will do. Just so you know, I'm actually championing you two. I think you'd make a great couple. I'm hoping she'll come around."

"Thank you, Paisley. Truth is, I know Nye thinks there's another woman, but there really isn't. It isn't like that. I want so much to tell her the truth, but she won't hear me out, so I don't know what more I can do right now."

"I've known her all my life; she'll come around, I'm sure of it."

Her tone is reassuring, but the look in her eyes doesn't quite agree with the words that came out of her mouth.

"What can I do, Paisley?"

"Give her time, Preston."

I try to smile, but it hurts too much.

"Thanks, Paisley. I'll see you around. Especially as you're dating my best friend."

She smiles, and this time it reaches her eyes. Her whole face lights up at the mere mention of Jack. And so it should. He's a good guy. One of the best.

As I leave the store, I feel dejected. Looking around, I see Christmas decorations going up everywhere. This town sure gets into the festive spirit—and who wouldn't when the town name itself is synonymous with the season—but I feel empty. Void of any Christmas spirit, like Ebenezer Scrooge.

If this is what women do to you, maybe I'm better off single after all. But I refuse to give up on Nye. The gauntlet has been thrown down and now I have to make it up to her. I didn't really do anything wrong by going to the pub with Cordelia, but I did leave it a week before trying to speak to Nye. I shouldn't have done that, and I can see why I need to grovel on my knees.

We had such a wonderful day that Sunday, and I had hopes of a future full of more days like that. I need to hold onto that hope. If I don't have hope, then what do I have? Until the moment she tells me to my face that she doesn't want to know, then I have to hold onto the shred of hope, no matter how tiny it might be. But I can't help but feel like shit at the moment.

Until today, I didn't know it was possible to feel this way. Now I know how much it hurts, and I will do anything I can to make it right, to make this pain go away, for both of us. I want to take the pain away from Nye, which will, in turn, take my own misery away—I hope.

***

Drinking my usual tipple at the bar in Mistletoe & Wine, I'm glad I have Jack to talk to. He's got a shit-eating grin permanently etched on his face and I can tell that it's Paisley that put it there. She seems like a nice girl and I hope that she and Jack can settle down and be happy.

"You look like someone kicked your puppy," he says as he takes a swig of the expensive whiskey he likes putting on my tab.

"You would too, if you were me right now."

"Seriously dude, it isn't anything that can't be straightened out."

"I'm going to try, but what can I do when she refuses to see me?"

"Make her see you. Don't take no for an answer. Turn up at her house. I don't know, just do *something*—anything."

"Can we change the subject?"

"It just seems harsh that she would be so mad at you for not speaking to her for a week. You have a hectic schedule at work, especially this time of year. You didn't call her or see her—that was a mistake, yes, but not something completely unforgivable. Plus, you're not used to wanting more with a woman than a casual thing, so you aren't used to the attention women require."

"It's not just that, Jack. She saw me here with Cordelia and now she thinks I have another woman waiting in the wings," I reply, air quoting her words to me.

"Well, that's just daft. Cordelia and you? Pfft! What a joke."

"I know that and so do you, but Aneurin doesn't. She doesn't know my past. We don't know each other that intimately. It hasn't come up in conversation."

"Well, then it needs to. You need to make her aware of the truth of the matter. I told Paisley that you aren't dating Cordelia, but I didn't know this was why she was asking."

"Wait, Paisley asked you what?"

"She asked if you were dating—and I quote—the blonde from the bar the other night."

"So, Nye is aware we aren't dating?"

"I'm not sure, dude. All I know is, I told Paisley you weren't dating anyone. What she told Nye, I don't know, I haven't asked. But even if she did tell her that—which I can only assume she did, else why would she ask—Nye still doesn't have the whole picture. She's only got my word for it that there's nothing between you and that stuck-up bitch."

"Say it like it is, why don't you?!"

"Well, she is a stuck-up bitch. I don't like her. Never have, never will."

I take a swig of my whiskey, letting the smooth burn travel down my throat slowly.

"Women are confusing as hell. If she knows we're not dating, then what's her problem?"

"The lack of acknowledgment after the two of you slept together?! That's my best guess. You're not used to paying women attention and if you want a future with Nye—or any other woman for that matter— you really need to change that. Be more present, more aware of what they want."

"Then that's what I'll do."

I hop down from my stool at the bar and straighten my jacket and tie. Jack looks confused, but I don't care.

"That bottle is paid for, you might as well drink it. I have somewhere else to be."

"You do?"

I don't answer as I pull out my phone and call a cab.

It isn't until the driver asks me for an address that I realize I don't know it. What now?

Snowflake is a small town, and everybody knows everybody else. I need to find someone who would be willing to tell me where Nye lives. I can't ask Paisley because she advised me to give Nye time and it hasn't even been a full day. But if Nye is this angry at me after one week of not talking, then she'll get even madder the longer I leave it, surely?! That's my reasoning and that's what I'll tell her if I can find someone to tell me where to find her.

I spot a woman I saw Nye with the other day. I don't know her name, but I tell the driver to pull over and wait for me.

Walking up to the woman, I pull my shoulders back and keep my head up, plastering a smile on my face and trying to keep my appearance friendly.

"Hi, umm… I'm sorry, I don't know your name. I'm a friend of Nye's," I say as I come to a stop in front of her.

"Oh, hi. I'm Trina."

I hold my hand out to her to shake, the only thing I can think to do. I realize with a jolt how much better Nye's hand feels enveloped in mine.

"I'm sorry to bother you like this, it's just that I seem to have lost her address. Is there any chance you could tell me where she lives?"

"Could you not call her and ask? I'm not sure I should be giving her address to a stranger."

"I would, but it's meant to be a surprise."

"Oh, well… umm…"

"I'm sorry, where are my manners? I'm Preston Fitzgerald."

My name seems to register as she smiles at me, recognition—of my name at least—flashing in her eyes.

"I'm sorry, I didn't recognize you, Mr. Fitzgerald."

"That's okay, I don't know everyone in town by name yet."

Trina smiles at me and reaches into her bag. She pulls a scrap of paper out along with a pen and scribbles something before handing it over.

"Thank you, Trina. I truly appreciate it. I'd also be in your debt if you didn't let her know I'm coming. I really want to surprise her."

"Sure thing. I saw you in the bar the other night and she kept looking at you. That was you, right? It was dark, but I'm sure it was you sat at the bar."

"That's right, I was with a business associate."

The fact that she's also my ex doesn't need explaining. It's only a small lie by omission, after all. Cordelia does still work for the company, at least she does until her maternity leave. It's Nye I need to tell the whole truth to.

"Well, I won't tell her you're coming. I hope you two kids have fun."

Trina winks at me then smiles as she starts to walk away.

"Thank you, Trina. You're a star."

She blushes as she looks back at me.

"You're welcome. Tell her I said hi."

"Will do."

With that, I get back in the cab and give the driver the address.

When he pulls up, I pay the fare and realize my palms are sweaty. I tell him to keep the change as I get out of the car and stand in front of Nye's door.

Wiping my palms on my suit trousers, I take a deep breath and walk up to the door. I knock lightly and wait patiently.

Shock registers in Nye's eyes as she opens the door wearing what I can only assume are her pajamas. They're silky looking and I can see her curves as the purple material clings to her.

"What do you want?"

Her tone is brusque, and her arms are folded across her chest. She doesn't realize it, but she's giving me a better view of her breasts.

"Can I come in? I'd really rather not air my laundry standing on your doorstep."

Moving to one side, she ushers me in. She doesn't speak a word as she closes the door and walks ahead of me into the lounge.

I follow her like a naughty schoolboy going to the headmistress's office. My heart beats a staccato rhythm in my chest and I have to take a couple of deep breaths to keep me focused.

Once in the lounge, Nye offers me a seat in the armchair. I take it and loosen my tie a little, finding it harder to breathe. Her expression leaves me in no uncertainty that I am more than in the doghouse.

"I'm so sorry, Aneurin. More than you could possibly know."

I look around and see the flowers on an end table. At least she didn't throw them away. That's something, I guess.

"What's done is done and can't be undone," she remarks as she takes a seat on the couch.

"But it can be explained, if you let me. Please, Nye, I'm begging you here."

She sighs and relaxes back onto the couch.

"Say what you have to and then leave."

God, I hope she doesn't force me to leave the second the words leave my mouth. I didn't exactly expect her to be receptive, but I feel like an errant child being scolded.

I start off with an apology for not talking to her or seeing her for a week. I know it sounds feeble, but I tell her how busy the business gets at this time of year. Then I tell her how I'm no good at relationships, because I don't really have lasting ones. It feels like some lame-ass excuse, but I explain how I'm not used to the whole thing of keeping in contact and stuff. She laughs at me derisively. It's only what I deserve, so I take my knocks and brace myself to continue.

After I've explained who Cordelia is to me, shock is written across Nye's features.

"I slapped a pregnant woman," she gasps.

"You did what?"

Now it's my turn to be shocked. I didn't even know they'd spoken. Why would Nye slap Cordelia? Knowing Cordelia, it was something to do with her stuck-up attitude, but Nye doesn't strike me as the type to lay hands on anyone.

"I…I slapped her across the face…I…didn't know she was pregnant."

Tears begin to stream down Nye's face and she folds in on herself. I move to sit next to her and she doesn't reject me.

I wrap my arms around her and pull her to my chest. I inhale her intoxicating scent, feeling more at ease with things than I did an hour ago. But what she said…what she did…I'm shocked, I can't say otherwise. However, Nye wasn't to know she was pregnant.

"Shh, it's okay Nye."

I run my fingers through her hair and her sobs begin to ebb away slowly.

"I didn't know, Preston. How could I have known?"

"Shh, you weren't to know. It'll be okay."

Cordelia didn't tell me about the incident, so I'm wondering if it's because she was embarrassed or, knowing her, because she's planning her revenge in great detail.

"She…she pushed me too far. The things she said…that's why I hit her. I didn't think it through. I'm not a violent person. Truly, Preston, that isn't me. I'm not that person. But when she said I wasn't good enough for someone like you…"

I pull back and look her in the eye.

"She said what?"

"She said something about my breeding and I lost my temper," she says, air-quoting the word breeding. "I shouldn't have reacted the way I did, but she made out that I wasn't good enough for you. I've never been good enough for anyone, Preston, that much is true. So why you should be any different, I don't know. I thought that maybe it was time, maybe I was finally good enough. But her words put me right back there with my doubts and horrible thoughts about myself."

"I'm sorry she said that to you, Nye. She had no right. The truth is, she was always jealous of any woman that looked my way. She knew I didn't really do relationships. I was too busy. It was too easy to just hook up and then walk away. But we'd been together for three months when she fell pregnant. My grandfather wanted us to get married and do things—and I quote—the 'right' way. I was to be a man for once in my life and make an honest woman of her. No grandchild of his was going to be born out of wedlock. So anytime a woman so much as smiled at me, Cordelia's claws came out. She usually took it out on me. We argued a lot. Another reason we were wrong for each other."

"Did she get pregnant to trap you?" she asks, voicing my concerns from so long ago.

"I don't know. Her family came from money themselves, so she didn't need mine. But my grandfather thought it would be a good idea to align our families. Money and power, they were all that mattered to that man. I always swore to myself I'd be nothing like him. Yet here I am, pushing away the one woman who's ever broken through my walls and made me want more."

"I'm sorry for asking, I just wondered about her motive. I guess I'm just suspicious of people. A little cynical, maybe. But it's not my business, I shouldn't have asked."

"Honestly, I wondered about her motive myself. Let me tell you this, Nye—I am an open book. If you want to ask me anything, and I mean *anything* at all, then just ask. I'll never lie to you. That's not who I am."

"Cordelia warning me off you really hurt. I didn't want to tell you about it. Whatever she really is to you, she made it sound like either she was your girlfriend or she wanted to be. Women don't warn each other off unless they're jealous."

"I don't get it though, because she's meant to be happy. She's been seeing a guy called Blake and she's four months pregnant. So, why would she be jealous over my feelings for you?"

"Pregnancy hormones?" She tries to joke but it comes out as a bit of a sob.

I really wish she'd stop crying. Cordelia Madison is the kind of woman who, if she was angry at Nye for slapping her, she would have made it a point to tell me. In fact, if she was trying to keep the two of us apart, it doesn't make sense that she didn't tell me. I'd ask her, but I'd probably get some vague nonsensical answer. That's just the way she is: bitchy, flippant, derisive. Three reasons why we could never have lasted. I had a lucky escape the day I found out I didn't have to marry her.

It hurt to lose the baby, sure, but our relationship was one of convenience, not of love. We were together because she was pregnant, to save face for my family. My grandfather would never have accepted a bastard child. That's what he called the baby when he found out.

"No grandchild of Preston Fitzgerald I will be born a bastard. You will marry her because it's the right thing to do. If you didn't want to marry her, then getting her pregnant wasn't a wise move, young man," he'd said.

I get up and walk into the kitchen to get Nye a glass of water. Standing at the sink, I slip my phone out of my pocket and contemplate sending a text to Cordelia. Truth is, she'd probably either deny it or make it out to be something it isn't. If I had to choose who to believe, it would be Aneurin. I know I haven't known her for very long, but she's inherently more trustworthy than Cordelia.

Chapter Ten

Nye

Preston stayed with me last night. He was amazing. I know I didn't want to speak to him but when he turned up on my doorstep, I had this overwhelming urge to tell him everything and, in the end, I did. He didn't blame me for my actions when it came to Cordelia. He said she's frustrating at the best of times, never mind at the worst of times. He said she doesn't have normal claws, he thinks they're made of adamantium like Wolverine. I had to giggle when he said that. Just like that, the atmosphere lightened between the two of us and, after his explanation, I let go of my frustration at him.

He held me while I cried, soothed me by gently stroking my back and running his fingers through my hair. It felt natural, like he'd been doing it all my life.

When I was finally so tired I couldn't keep my eyes open, he said he'd call a cab home, but it was after midnight and if I'm being honest, I wanted him to hold me as I slept. He ended up in my bed in his boxer shorts and I was still in my silky purple pajamas. Nothing untoward happened, neither one of us pushing the other for something more. I mean, we kissed, but nothing more than that.

I crept down the stairs this morning and made him breakfast in bed. Only scrambled egg on toast, but I didn't know what else he liked.

Now I'm sitting on the bed watching him. His face is relaxed in sleep and he looks different, lighter somehow. It's almost like when he's awake he assumes the weight of his job and all that entails. Yet when he's asleep, none of those things are bothering him. The pressure he's under vanishes without a trace.

He rolls onto his side and opens his eyes. Taking in the sight of me, he smiles a sleepy but sexy smile. I find myself thinking that this is what he could look like every morning.

"Good morning," I say as I hold out his mug of strong black coffee. It isn't as expensive as what he drinks at home, but I think it's nice all the same.

"Good morning," he replies as he moves to sit up and take the mug.

I can't help but stare at the hard planes of his body, remembering what they feel like under my touch. He catches me staring and I feel a blush creep across my chest, on to my neck and up to warm my cheeks.

"See something you like?" he asks in a husky voice.

"No."

His shocked gasp comes with a hand across his heart, feigning hurt.

"That's a pity, Miss Mackenzie, as I see something I like, very much so."

I watch his hooded gaze as it roams over my curves. My skin tingles like there's an electrical current between us. If you stay still enough, you can feel it crackle in the air.

Breaking the spell, I hand him his eggs.

"We don't want them getting cold."

"Honestly, eggs won't satiate my hunger, Aneurin," he says as he takes the plate from my hands.

We're getting into dangerous territory here. My body wants him more than the air I need to breathe, but my head tells me to do the sensible thing and play it cool. If he wants me, he'll have to work for it.

"Well then it's a good job there's toast on your plate too."

"You and I both know that isn't what I meant."

His husky voice is making my insides melt into a puddle of goo. So much for staying strong. Under his scrutiny, I can feel myself coming apart at the seams.

Deciding to completely break this hold he has over me, I get up and grab a towel. I walk into my en-suite, turn the water on and wait for it to warm up before stepping in.

"Fancy some company in there?"

"Nope, I'm good."

The look on my face in the mirror says otherwise, but thankfully he can't see that. Now I'm standing here squeezing my thighs together, trying to quell the feelings beginning to stir within me.

"You sure?"

I want to give in, but I can't. If he wants something more with me than a casual hook-up, like he's admitted most women have been to him in the past, then what we could have isn't going to start with sex. Even if I know he gives mind-blowing orgasms. Even if I know his lips set my skin on fire. Even if I know how it feels to have him inside me—and it feels incredible. No, I need to retain some dignity and keep him at arm's length, for now at least.

Instead of answering, I strip and step under the spray of water. Standing there, I let it wash over me and take with it all traces of last night, the last week and all thoughts of Cordelia. I'll need to make an apology to her at some point, but that can wait.

Afterward, I wrap myself up in a towel with another around my hair. I walk into the bedroom to be greeted with the sight of Preston bending over, pulling his trousers on. He has a great ass. Toned and firm. Buns of steel. I really need to pull my mind out of the gutter, but his lean body makes it difficult. As he stands, I look at his broad back. His muscles and definition are simply perfection. He's not overly ripped and muscular, but he has the finest physique of any man I've ever had the pleasure of seeing naked in the flesh. He has a body made for sin.

The tightening in my abdomen tells me that I want him more than I am letting on. I feel desire swirling around inside and my tongue darts out to wet my bottom lip. As he turns to face me, my eyes drop to that defined V and my mind is definitely stuck in the gutter. I'm thinking of tracing that V with my fingers and then with my tongue. My hand reaches out as if it has a mind of his own, but I stop myself short.

Preston laughs, and I know I've been caught. It was impossible for him to miss my hand darting out, but I had hoped he'd be enough of a gentleman not to draw attention to it.

"Still not seeing anything you like?" he asks with a chuckle.

"Nope. Nothing. There's nothing to see here."

I wander across my room and grab some clean clothes. It looks like I'm going to be a little late for work, so I grab my phone and tap out a quick text to Paisley. She responds immediately telling me not to worry, it's not like it's busy at this time of the morning.

I turn around to see Preston watching me, hunger making his eyes light up.

"Would you mind turning around?" I ask, as though he hasn't seen it all before.

I know he's seen me naked already, but, although we haven't really discussed it, this feels like a fresh start.

He walks out of the room and gives me the privacy to get dressed. Once I've pulled on a sweater and skinny jeans, I find my Converse and slip my feet into them. They aren't exactly shiny and new, they're actually rather worn in, but that's just me. I prefer comfort over anything. I may run a clothing boutique and I may dress nicely to fit an occasion, but on a day to day basis, I just wear what I'm comfortable in.

I walk out of my room and nearly trip over Preston as he's sitting on the top step of the staircase.

He gets up and we go downstairs in silence. I'm not sure whether he's got his guard back up again, but there's something different about the feeling in the air.

"I ought to go home to shower and change before going to work," he says as we stand in my kitchen.

"Are you okay?"

I don't want to push him, but his mood seems to have soured pretty quickly.

"I was just thinking about what a crazy bitch Cordelia is and how to resolve the situation. She needs to know I'm not okay with her speaking to you that way."

"I lashed out at her, Preston. I was more in the wrong than she was."

"You've admitted that, and I can see how sorry you are. But she needs to confess her part in it too. I won't have her walking around thinking she can act that way. She knew I liked you, I told her that night. She's acting like a jealous, crazy woman and I won't stand for it."

"I'd like to apologize to her."

He looks at me and smiles.

"I have an idea. I'll ask her to meet me. Not somewhere public, I don't want her causing a scene. But when she turns up, you and I will both be there, and we can try to clear the air. What do you say?"

"Just let me know when and where."

His smile widens, and he crosses the distance between us to wrap his arms around me.

"I care about you, Nye. I want the air cleared so that we can properly start afresh if that's what you want?"

"Of course I do."

I'd love nothing more than a fresh start with this gorgeous man who makes me feel all kinds of happy.

Chapter Eleven

Preston

I've been working all morning and Cordelia has yet to return my call. I left her a voicemail asking if she could give me a ring. If she doesn't respond, my only option will be to go to her house, although I don't want it to feel like Nye and I are ambushing her. But I'd much rather piss her off than Nye. I want to be considerate of both of their feelings, but that will depend on Cordelia.

My phone rings half an hour later.

"What can I do for you, Preston?" Cordelia says in that saccharine sweet voice she seems to reserve for the male of the species.

"I know you're meant to be working out of the office today and I apologize for interrupting, but we need to talk."

"About?"

"I'd rather not say over the phone. Can you come to the office in an hour?"

"Hmm…I can do two thirty, is that okay?"

"Great. See you then."

"Okay, see you shortly."

The call disconnects and I realize I probably came off as quite rude. I guess I was a little terse, but I don't like the woman and don't like needing to talk to her for any reason. I actually go out of my way to avoid her like the plague.

I send a text to Nye, asking her to meet me at the office a little before Cordelia is set to arrive. She quickly replies with an "Okay". Safe to say she's not exactly looking forward to it either.

Work keeps my mind occupied until my receptionist buzzes the intercom at two o'clock. I walk to the front desk and greet Nye with a chaste kiss. She looks beautiful, as always. Dressed in a knitted jumper, skinny jeans and a pair of Converse, one might think she looks kind of out of place in a swanky place like this building. But if I'm being honest,

I am caring less and less about the designer labels and the fancy clothes. Nye must be rubbing off on me.

I tell her about the phone call and that I may have been a little curt with Cordelia when really, I should have been keeping her sweet so that she'd be more open to an apology from Nye. But since I didn't actually mention that the reason I wanted her here involved Nye, I'm hoping it won't matter.

At two thirty on the dot, Jenny buzzes the intercom again, alerting me to Cordelia's punctual arrival.

Greeting her in reception, I get a hint of her usual vanilla scent as she air kisses my cheek. It's nowhere near as appealing as the scent of Nye, which is strawberries and cream and something that's uniquely her own.

"Preston, may I ask what this is about?" she asks as we approach my office door.

"Let's just get inside the office, it's not a conversation I want the rest of the staff overhearing."

She walks into the office ahead of me and stops abruptly, almost making me trip behind her.

"What's this?"

Cordelia gestures towards Nye and turns to look at me with what I've come to know as her resting bitch face. Thank you, Nye, for teaching me that look actually has a name.

"Don't blame Preston," Nye chimes in. "This is my doing. I didn't think you'd show up if I was the one to ask."

"Why don't we take a seat, Cordelia?"

I gesture towards the comfortable leather chairs to one side of my office.

She gives me a funny look but takes a seat anyway. Nye joins us and the three of us are seated just as there is a knock at my door.

Once Jenny leaves to make a pot of coffee, I'm left with just the two women facing off against each other. It seems like a childhood staring contest, first one to blink loses. I feel uncomfortable, never normally having to be in this kind of situation. But if Nye is going to be in my life, then I need to get used to being outside of my comfort zone.

"I wanted to apologize," Nye begins, once Jenny has brought in the coffee and closed the door. "I owe you a huge apology, Cordelia."

Cordelia just stares at her without batting an eyelid.

"And just what do you wish to apologize for, Aneurin?"

Her cold tone is enough to make a normal person shrink in their seat, but Nye looks calm and in control.

"I slapped you, and that is something that should never have happened. I'm not that type of person and I certainly didn't know you were pregnant, otherwise, I would never have laid a hand on you."

I see Cordelia place a hand on her flat stomach, protective of her unborn child.

"I don't know what I can do to make it up to you, Cordelia. I don't know that anything can make up for it, but I am truly sorry. Sorrier than you could know."

Seeing tears form in her eyes, I reach my hand out to Nye. She takes it and I relax a little in my seat.

"You're right, it never should have happened. You had no right to do what you did, whether I am pregnant or not. Violence never solves anything. But you're right, you slapped a pregnant woman and I don't know whether I can forgive and forget."

"I know that, I really do. But I will grovel on my hands and knees if that's what it takes."

A wicked glint in Cordelia's eyes tells me she'd like nothing more than to see Nye on her knees, begging forgiveness.

I'm about to jump in and stop that from happening, but at the last moment I realize it isn't needed. Nye can fight her own battles. She told me she wanted to do this, and I told her how Cordelia would be likely to react. She knows that Cordelia has a heart of stone and won't just forgive her and act like nothing ever happened.

"That won't be necessary. Truth be told, I said some things I shouldn't have said."

There's a sharp intake of breath, too loud for the quiet in the room. It takes a moment, but I suddenly realize it came from me.

"We both did things that we shouldn't have. In the spirit of being honest, it isn't entirely out of character for me to act the way I did, but it was churlish and I apologize."

"I agree, we both did something we shouldn't have. You judged a book by its cover when you looked at me and said I wasn't good enough for Preston. You shouldn't have made such assumptions. But there was no way I should have slapped you for what you said. It was a knee-jerk reaction, but two wrongs don't make a right. That's why I'm here, why

Preston asked you to be here today... I wanted to make it clear that I am apologetic and it's not just because you're pregnant either. I shouldn't have laid hands on you either way."

Looking at Nye, I see a beautiful, composed, articulate woman. She's made Cordelia do something I have never seen or heard her do before—apologize. That takes some doing. I have never been able to do it. Neither has anyone I've ever come across.

"Then I suggest we both try to forgive, let it go and move on."

Wow. I totally didn't see that coming. I guess you really shouldn't make assumptions about someone. Okay, so Cordelia has never admitted wrongdoing in the past, but you can't always judge a person on their past. Some people really are capable of change.

"Thank you, Cordelia. I really am very sorry, and I promise nothing like that will ever happen again. Ever."

"Then consider it forgiven. We both own our mistakes, right? So, do you agree we should let it lie? We need never mention it again."

"Agreed."

Cordelia reaches out to take her—probably cold—coffee from the table and smiles at Nye. Maybe leopards can change their spots after all. Maybe.

When she stands, Cordelia reaches out to shake Nye's hand. They both silently convey again how sorry they are for their actions. Then as quickly as she breezed in, Cordelia is on her way.

Nye and I sit for a while, neither of us voicing any concerns that Cordelia may not let the past rest. I see the mistrust in her eyes for a fleeting moment, but then it's gone, replaced by those sparkling green gems I am used to gazing into.

As I see Nye out of the building, I lean in to kiss her lightly on the lips, but she puts her arms around my neck and pulls me close. Our lips lock and our tongues duel for dominance over a breath-stealing kiss. If I wasn't outside of my place of work, it's the kind of kiss that would make a tent in my trousers, and I'd probably whisk Nye away to take it further. But I regain my composure as she pulls away and smiles at me.

One heartwarming smile and I'm a goner. She's everything I never knew I needed. A breath of fresh air in a life that has been far too stale for far too long.

***

My hair is a disheveled mess by the end of the day, having run my fingers through it in frustration so many times. There is always so much more to be done around Christmas. All I want is some free time to spend with Nye. I want to get to know her better. But there don't seem to be enough hours in the day. If I wasn't such a workaholic and could delegate some of my workload to my assistant, maybe I'd have some more time on my hands, but I've never been comfortable with someone else being in control.

Call me a control freak, but I like to be the one in charge. I like things done a certain way and that means personally overseeing things that my assistant should be able to handle; that's why I employed him after all.

Frustrated at the crappy day I've had, I decide to call it a night and head home. I need something to put a smile on my face, so I text Nye:

Preston: Hey, gorgeous. How's your day been?

I see the three dots bouncing as she types a reply.

Nye: Busy, busy, busy. What about you?

Preston: Stressful.

Nye: Fancy a drink in the pub? Just a quick one if you're busy.

I feel a smile tug at my lips.

Preston: Sure, just let me pop home and change. I feel like this tie is trying to strangle the life out of me.

Nye: Okay. Should we say an hour?

Preston: That would be great. See you then xx

And just like that, my crappy day has been put to the back of my mind.

***

Sitting in a booth with Nye, I see and hear the hustle and bustle of people getting ready for Christmas. Outside, I can see people carrying trees to their cars from the tree lot just across the street. Families looking happy as they've chosen the perfect one for their home.

It makes me realize that I don't even own a tree or any decorations. No traditional family ornaments handed down through the generations. My family were always too busy at this time of year. It was a hugely busy time for the business, so real life got pushed to one side until the new year. Not that much changed when January rolled around. It saddens me that I spend Christmas one of two ways—I'm either working or I'm home alone. I don't bother cooking a proper Christmas dinner either, I just cook whatever I fancy or whatever I happen to have in the fridge.

Could this Christmas be different? I don't want to infringe on any plans Nye might have, but in my mind's eye, I can see us spending time together. We could be really happy, especially if Cordelia disappears the way she came.

"What are your plans this Christmas?" she asks, as though she's read my mind.

"Probably up to my eyeballs in work."

"Do you ever do anything but work? You do know that work would still be there afterward if you decided to take a few days off."

"I guess it's just the way it's always been. I've never known proper family Christmases since my father died. My mother tried, but her efforts were always in vain because his absence was far too noticeable. My grandfather didn't care a bit for Christmas. He was the epitome of Scrooge. When I came to work with him, I learned to just work, work, work. We didn't bother with the festive period at all except to help the businesses we invested in."

"How old were you when your father died?"

I don't answer immediately, and Nye reaches her hand across the table to wrap around mine.

"I'm sorry, Preston. Forget I asked. I shouldn't have said anything."

"I was fifteen. It was awful. He died of a heart attack and I was the one who found him. I was home alone with him while my mother did her Christmas shopping. I needed to go to the toilet, so I knocked on the door, thinking he was in the shower. I was being lazy and couldn't be bothered to walk down to the next level of the house. He didn't answer, so I assumed he was in his room. I opened the door and that was when I saw him on the floor. I tried CPR, but it was no use. I called for an ambulance and then called my mother to come home. I've never been so scared in my entire life."

"Oh my gosh, I am so sorry Preston."

I see her eyes shining with unshed tears. My own eyes sting as I try to hold back the tears that I haven't shed in the last fifteen years. My father wasn't around to see me turn eighteen and become the man he always wanted me to be. He wasn't there to see me graduate. Neither was he there to see me take the helm of the family business—even though that's something I never wanted to do—when his father passed away. There's so much he missed out on. And there's so much wisdom of his that I missed out on over the years.

"It's okay, Nye, it was a long time ago," I reply, even though it feels like only yesterday.

"We were meant to come here and have a drink to forget your work troubles, not bring up more. I'm so sorry I mentioned it."

I look into her emerald gaze and see sympathy.

"It's all part of getting to know one another. If we hadn't discussed it now, we would have another time."

Squeezing her hand, I smile at her and see her shoulders relax infinitesimally. I want to make her smile, to laugh, not to cry or to worry about me. So, instead of sitting here wallowing, I take her hand and lead her to the dancefloor.

"On This Winter's Night" by Lady Antebellum begins to play, so I hold Nye in my arms and dance slowly. Singing softly in her ear, I sweep her gently across the dancefloor.

When the song is over, I lean down and place a chaste kiss on Nye's lips. She smells like strawberries and it's enough to hypnotize me. Her arms release from around my neck and she takes my hand as she leads me back to our booth.

"What do you say we get out of here?" she asks.

"Where to?"

"I don't know, anywhere but here."

"How would you feel about helping me pick out a tree?"

"You don't have your tree yet? All the best ones will be gone. You're cutting it a bit fine, Mr. Fitzgerald."

"I'm sure you could help me make even a not-so-brilliant tree look amazing. Yours looks fantastic."

"Oh, you noticed that?"

"I couldn't help it. It's a big tree. Bright and beautiful with tasteful decorations."

"Thank you."

She blushes at the compliment as she grabs her bag, so we can head out.

As we head over to the tree lot, Nye holds my hand like it's the most natural thing in the world. Maybe it is. I'm just not used to affection in small or large displays.

***

Once the tree is in place, Nye smiles at me and it lights her eyes. I feel a large grin take over my own features and it feels good.

Nye asked me if I want to shop for decorations tomorrow and though there is so much work to be done, I immediately canceled my entire schedule for the day, pushing meetings back, so that I can spend the day in her company. She's incredible and she makes me feel something I didn't know I could feel. I want to spend as much time with her as physically possible and that is the opposite of how I usually am with women, so it feels strange, yet so natural at the same time.

A barrage of questions comes to mind. How can I be falling so far, so soon? Does she feel the same? Is this thing between us the real thing? Can I commit to someone I barely know? There's so much more we need to know about each other, but we've discussed the essentials and it actually feels like I've known her forever rather than just a few months. But in all reality, we haven't known each other *this* well up until now, so are we rushing in too fast? The most important question in my head at the moment though is: will Nye take care of my heart if I give it to her?

The heart wants what it wants, and I don't want to deny the way I feel. Plus, I feel like I can trust Nye not to hurt me. She's been hurt herself and I'm sure she wouldn't intentionally hurt anyone else, much less me. But I need to know she feels the same before we go too much further. That's the control freak in me, I think. Maybe a tad of anxiety over the fact that I've never wanted to feel like this about anyone up until now and now I have no control over where my heart is leading me.

Chapter Twelve

Nye

It's bright and early with a crisp December air. My coat is pulled tightly around me, and I have on my warmest boots.

I promised Preston a day of Christmas shopping for decorations for his tree and his home and that is exactly what he's going to get. I'm going to show him that, sometimes, money isn't everything.

He proposed the idea of buying all his decorations online, paying extra for expedited delivery. I soon put the kibosh on that idea. There's nothing like seeing the decorations up close and getting a feel for them, for whether they are right for you. Pictures on the internet can be deceptive, even with as much money as he has and the ability to shop in the best places.

I'm sitting waiting for Preston to arrive. I said I'd drive us around town because my car is more inconspicuous, so he's getting a cab over to me. I did offer to pick him up, but he said he didn't want me to go out of my way, driving to the edge of town to get him and then back into town to shop.

At nine thirty sharp, there's a knock on the door.

Dressed in a pair of indigo jeans, a pair of black leather boots, and a bomber jacket done up against the breeze, he looks like he's just stepped out of the pages of a glossy magazine. His hair is tousled, not neatly styled like it is when he's at work. I love the casual look on him. I mean, sure, his casual clothes probably still cost more than my best clothes, but he looks incredible.

He walks in and I inhale a deep lungful of the sandalwood cologne he's wearing. He looks me up and down, assessing my choice in clothing, then smiles.

"Good morning, beautiful," he says as he stands leaning against the wall with his ankles crossed.

"Good morning, Preston."

"Please, by now I'm sure we can be less formal. I call you Nye, after all, even though I adore your full name."

"So, what should I call you? Do you have a nickname?"

"Wolf."

I can't help the giggle that escapes me.

"Is that because you're a predator, or does it signify other...umm... appetites?"

His deep rumble of laughter is music to my ears. He really needs to laugh more often.

"It's from my middle name, Wolfric. It's what the other boys called me at boarding school. But yes, I guess you could say it's appropriate for my other appetites too."

I try to stifle my giggles but fail spectacularly. I laugh until my sides hurt and I'm wrapping my arms around them as though I might fall apart.

Preston also laughs so deeply. An utterly delightful sound if ever I heard one.

"Should we get going, Wolf?" I ask before giggling again.

"Lead the way, little lamb," he says in a foreboding voice.

"Hey, I'm no lamb. I'm more like a tiger...a tigress? Is that the right word? It reminds me of the character from Kung Fu Panda."

Preston laughs, though whether it's because of my naiveté or my Disney reference, I don't know.

"Actually, you can call a female either a tiger or a tigress."

"Good to know."

I chuckle as I grab my bag ready to go.

***

After shopping for a couple of hours, we stop for lunch. Preston has insisted on eating in a cozy little pub just on the outskirts of town. Why? Because it's called The White Lion, which he found incredibly funny, given our earlier conversation about predators and prey. I nudged him in the ribs and told him not to be such a dick. He just laughed at me, took me by the hand and led me inside.

We have quite the haul of decorations, but Preston has told me he doesn't have a keen eye for interior design, so he's asked me if I'll help.

Of course, I've said yes because it means spending more time together. I'd do anything to spend more time in his company.

Having talked about everything and nothing, I feel like I have a better sense of who he is. He's charming, funny, intelligent, sarcastic and has a wicked sense of humor. He's pretty much everything I look for in a man. From just one look at him, you might think he's just some rich asshole that likes to look good, and maybe you might think he's arrogant, cocky, bigheaded. But if you look beneath the surface, you see his heart of gold.

I wasn't looking for a relationship when I met him and if someone had told me that I'd end up starting to have feelings for him, I would have laughed in their face. I thought he was all those things, cocky and arrogant most of all. However, the longer I spend in his company, the more I realize he's warm, caring, kind, generous and a whole lot else besides.

Could I be starting to develop feelings for him? At this stage, it could go either way. I know how I feel, but I don't want to voice that to him in case he doesn't see us the same way. It isn't love…yet. But there's hope and possibility of that in the future. Or at least there is for me. Could this alpha wolf be developing the same type of feelings for me? Only time will tell.

***

I'm sitting amidst a myriad of colorful boxes containing assorted ornaments, tinsel, a garland for the fireplace, and strings of lights. The Christmas tree is in a corner of the lounge, taking up all the room that one corner had to offer. It was one of few trees left at the tree lot, because it was more expensive than the others and I guess it was rather too large for most people to take home. Preston paid extra for Dalton to deliver it, as he wasn't going to strap it to the top of the car. He didn't want to scratch my car, which I found sweet.

Once it arrived, the two men set to work bringing it inside and trying it out in various positions before settling on where it is now.

The sunlight will stream through the windows in the mornings and it will look beyond magical in here by the time I am finished.

Preston—I still refuse to refer to him as Wolf because it's too amusing—is making hot chocolate while I sort out the decorations.

I pointed out a beautiful tree topper when we were shopping—an angel wearing a beautiful burgundy dress.

Looking at the box in front of me, I see some blown glass ornaments that had caught Preston's eye, but he said he had no idea how they would fit in with the theme. I accepted the unspoken challenge, so here I am, trying to plan out where they should go.

The rich, chocolatey aroma catches my attention and I look up to see Preston smiling down at me. He's holding two mugs of steaming hot chocolate, topped with squirty cream, chocolate shavings and mini-marshmallows. My mouth waters at the sight and smell.

"One hot chocolate, as promised," he says as he places them on the end table closest to me.

"It's thirsty work, all this tree decorating."

"Umm…" he trails off as he looks at the bare tree.

"I know, I know," I say as I wave my hands around at the boxes. "There's an art to it and the design is all coming together in my head."

"Oh, right." He sounds unconvinced.

"I swear, I have it all planned out. I was just about to make a start when I smelled the rich aroma of chocolate. So, really, it's your fault for distracting me from the task at hand."

His chest rumbles with laughter. I'm not sure whether to be insulted by his laughter or whether to join in. I pout at him, crossing my arms and pretending I'm insulted. He laughs harder and I can't help but break out into a smile of my own.

***

The last thing to go on the tree is, of course, the topper. Preston holds me around the waist as he lifts me easily—as though I weigh no more than a feather—to put it in place.

I place the angel and feel my feet touch the floor. Making no attempt to release my waist, Preston instead pulls me closer, my back to his chest, and his arms wrap around me.

I can feel his heart pounding, mirroring the rhythm of my own. The scent of his cologne wraps around my senses, invading every empty space inside me, filling it up with him and only him. If he wasn't holding me up, I'd probably swoon at his feet. My heart feels full to bursting.

His breathing tickles my back as he leans down to kiss the side of my neck. Butterflies take flight in my stomach as his soft lips make their way down to my shoulder. He moves my sweater from my shoulder and places tender kisses across my skin. Desire swirls inside and it's all I can do not to tear the clothes from his body.

I turn in his embrace, and wrap my arms around his neck as he dips low to ghost a kiss over my lips. The hunger inside me is bursting to be free. I want him to fill my body as much as he does my heart and mind.

His lips claim mine once more in a punishing kiss. Matching his intensity, I give myself over to him. His tongue dances with mine as I realize how addictive his taste is. It's like a drug and I'm the junkie, strung out on its effects.

Hands roam my body, from my waist, to my ribcage and up to my breasts. I reach around and unclip my bra, showing him that I want his touch on me, underneath my clothes the way he's already underneath my skin.

His deft hands move to tease my nipples and I inhale sharply as they pebble at his touch. His touch sets me on fire, burning me up like a match to gasoline. A warmth pools in my abdomen as he kisses down to the swell of my breasts. Looking into my eyes, Preston must see the permission he seeks, before he dips back down to take my nipple in his warm mouth, covering the bud and his teeth gently nipping it before he moves to lavish the other with the same attention.

If it weren't for his embrace keeping me together, I would be a pool of jelly, my bones liquified by his intensity.

Sensual kisses pepper my skin to the hollow of my throat and up across my jaw. His lips slant over mine and he kisses me fervently.

My hands go to the hem of his t-shirt and slip softly underneath. I trace the hard lines of his body as if they are a road map to heaven itself. Dipping below the waistband of his jeans, I hear him sharply inhale as he waits for my next move. I cup his stiffening cock in the palm of my hand and I gently stroke up and down over the material of his boxer shorts. His breathing becomes labored in my ear as he dips to gently nip my earlobe.

I don't know if I've ever wanted another person as much in my life as I want Preston right now.

Feeling bold, I slip my hand underneath his boxer shorts. A moan escapes Preston as he feels my skin connect with his. Feeling him grow harder, I stroke the length of him, gripping firmly. My heart beats frantically as I trace my thumb around him using the pre-cum on his tip.

Looking around, I see the armchair not far behind Preston and I edge him closer to it. Once I have him where I want him, I move to undo his zipper, and slip the material down over his hips. It's a good job he lives so far back from the neighborhood, else we'd be giving them a good show, considering his curtains are wide open and the windows are almost floor to ceiling.

I push him to sit down and grip him in my hand once more as I settle down on my knees in between his outstretched legs. He discards his jeans and boxer shorts to one side.

Taking just the tip of him in my mouth, I hear a groan reverberate through his chest. His hand goes to the back of my hair, pulling it out of the way so he can see what I am doing to him.

My hand and mouth in sync, I work him over slowly, building a rhythm and creating a frenzied feeling within me. I've never felt a lust so strong or an attraction so unfathomable as this before.

Before I get a chance to protest, I feel weightless as Preston lifts me easily from the floor. He holds me with one arm behind my knees and the other cradling my back. Walking out of the lounge, he heads for the stairs. My head is cradled against his chest and I feel his heart beating just as wildly as my own.

We enter his bedroom and he lays me down on his bed reverently. He kneels between my legs and kisses the apex of my thigh before dipping lower and licking me languorously, almost as if he's afraid I'll fall apart if he goes any quicker. My chest rises and falls rapidly, my heart and head full of carnal desire for this man: this cocky, arrogant, yet perfect man. I never intended to feel anything for him, but I can't deny what I now know to be true; I am no longer falling. I fell before I knew what was happening to me. Now my only choice is to either go with it or run for the hills.

As his finger slowly slips inside me, my thighs begin to quiver. My back arches off the bed as he moves inside me. A small moan escapes my lips as he begins to find his rhythm. He doesn't know it yet, but it isn't just my body he is bending to his will…it's all of me. Every single fiber of my being is calling out for him to own it. To dominate it. To mark it as his for life. Maybe that sounds crazy, and it even feels it, but that doesn't mean to say that crazy is a bad thing. In this case, it's a beautiful thing. He's marking my soul as part of his own. If he were to leave now, that part would leave with him. There would be a hole in my soul that could never be mended, save for him coming back to me. I feel mad just for thinking these things, but it's my heart talking, not my brain; that's the one organ that would try and talk me out of how I feel. At least it might, if it was thinking coherently right now.

Passion burns through me and I cry out his name as my body falls over the edge and into the abyss. Satiated, but still hungry. That's how it feels to be me right now. The only thing to do now is to wait for my body to recover before I stake my claim on him the way he just did with me.

Chapter Thirteen

Preston

I'm rock hard as she strokes me, over and over. She's enough to drive a sane man crazy. I want her more than I've ever wanted another woman. Cordelia never drove me to the edge of my own sanity in this way. Sure, she drove me crazy, but not in the bedroom. Nye, however, seems to control every atom of my body. My blood runs white hot through my veins as she straddles me and leans down to claim my lips in a searing kiss.

My hands roam up and down her sides, stopping to cup her breasts as my fingers trace a circle around her nipples. They pebble instantly, and it only serves to make my cock harder.

Nye's hands run over my pecs, down over every hard line of my body to the V she loves to touch so much. Her back arches as I slip one hand down to play with her clit. She's wet already from me feasting on her and her falling apart. I have never heard a sound as sexy as the one she made as the orgasm tore through her body and washed over me in waves. She tasted glorious, like something I want to keep experiencing every single day until the day I die. It's a strange feeling for me, wanting more from her than any other woman I've ever met. But I can't control what my heart desires, even though I didn't think I was capable of feeling this way. I don't want to scare her off with those three little words yet, but it doesn't mean I can't think them every time I'm with her.

Pulling me out of my own thoughts, Nye slides her hand between us and guides the tip of me inside her. It feels…inexplicable. My balls tighten as her warmth envelopes me. I suddenly feel like I've forgotten what to do. All sense has left me.

Nye's hips start to buck against me and my cock throbs with need.

Her scent swirls around me and I inhale a deep breath. She's intoxicating, spellbinding, exquisite.

My hands reach for her hips as she splays her hands on my chest. As her back arches, a moan escapes those pretty lips and it takes all my resolve not to fall apart underneath her.

Leaning down, she claims my lips in a bruising kiss as she continues to rock her hips against me. I reach up to cup her breasts, making her hiss out a sharp breath as I tease one nipple between my forefinger and thumb.

Breaking our kiss, I lean in and gently nip her nipple between my teeth. Her back arches and her movements falter as she lets out a deep groan of satisfaction. Moving to pay her other nipple the same attention, I hold her hips as she moves up and down, her rhythm increasing.

My heart feels as though it's going to break free from its constraints. I can feel it pounding heavily, begging to be set free.

"Preston, I…"

She doesn't finish her thought as I buck my hips to meet her every thrust. Her nails dig into my shoulders, marking me as hers. I wouldn't want to be anyone else's.

"Let go, baby," I whisper.

Her hair flows wildly around her shoulders and her eyes are a deep emerald green. She looks incredible as her rhythm begins to falter. I hold her tightly as she comes undone. Her chest rises and falls rapidly as she cries out. My balls tighten, and I feel an intense tingling sensation as I reach my own climax.

Nye falls against me, her arms no longer strong enough to hold her up and I cradle her against my chest as my breathing slowly returns to normal.

I feel her heartbeat pounding, her chest heaving against mine. Running my hands through her hair, I'm held captive by this amazing woman. I want to fall asleep with her in my arms every night and wake to her beautiful face every morning. Could this really be love that I'm feeling? If it is, then why isn't it as scary as I thought it would be?

Drifting off to sleep, I think of what a future with Nye could hold. We'd make such beautiful babies. Wait…we'd what? Where did that come from?

***

I wake still holding Nye. She's asleep with her head on my chest, her body flush to my side and her leg thrown across mine.

Taking the time to really look at her, my gaze wonders over her curves. Her creamy skin feels soft as I stroke a hand up and down her back.

As she begins to stir, her face tilts towards mine and I watch as her eyes slowly open. Her lips curve into a sleepy, sexy smile.

"Morning," she says sleepily.

"Good morning."

I don't want to let go of her yet. I don't want to burst the bubble we created last night.

Nye stretches out lazily, not showing any signs of hurrying to be free of whatever this is between us. I watch unabashedly as she works out the kinks in her lithe body. Her hand comes up to trace the muscles of my chest as I lie here, delighting in her touch.

Her lips quickly replace where her fingers have been, and she throws me a salacious grin as she works her way down my chest. A feeling stirs within me and I want to show her that last night wasn't a one-time deal to me—okay so technically it was the second time we've slept together, but I want to show her that it's not just about sex with her. I want more, so much more. And I want to show her there's more to me than meets the eye. I'm not just some cocky asshole who screws women and discards them—not anymore, anyway—I'm capable of feelings, emotions. There's something tangible between us, something real. I want her to explore this side of me and get to know me better.

***

After working up an appetite, I offered to cook Nye breakfast. She's sitting at my granite kitchen island as I cook bacon and eggs. I'm humming to myself and feeling blissfully happy. None of this "waiting for the other shoe to drop" thing. I'm living in the moment with a beautiful woman, knowing that what I feel for her is becoming more real by the second. I have the sense that she might just reciprocate what I feel, and I owe it to myself as well as her to explore this connection.

Plates cleared, Nye sits sipping coffee as I load the dishwasher. I clear my throat as I catch her staring at me. She blushes and averts her gaze.

I move to stand in front of her and put a finger under her chin, tilting it so that she's facing me.

"Don't ever feel ashamed if you're caught looking at me. Do you see me averting my gaze when you catch me looking at you?"

"Umm... no."

"That's because I'm not embarrassed at being caught. I look at you and I see the most beautiful woman I've ever seen. Why shouldn't I look at you?"

She remains quiet and I see a rosy blush creep across her skin.

"Let's just settle this right now," I say with a smile. "You can look at me all you want, and you don't have to be embarrassed about it."

The sound of her phone ringing stops me from saying more. I glance down at the counter and see Paisley's name flash on her phone screen.

"I'll leave you to take your call. I guess I ought to get dressed anyway," I say, before kissing the top of her head and walking away.

Once in my room, I grab a towel and head for my en-suite. I need a cold shower as her appraisal of my body has left me with a stiff cock. The way she bit that bottom lip made me recall how it felt having her mouth wrapped around my cock this morning. God how she felt when she licked and sucked me like no other woman ever has. I hadn't been able to hold off for too long before coming in hot spurts down her throat. She'd licked me clean and then crawled up my body to kiss me. I'd tasted myself on her—such an erotic thing to experience.

Now I'm standing to attention in the shower, wishing Nye was here in front of me on her knees. I can faintly hear her chatting to Paisley downstairs, so I take hold of myself and close my eyes. Pumping up and down gently at first, I feel a tingling travel down my spine. Remembering how wet and tight Nye feels wrapped around me, I jerk a little faster, adjusting my grip a little tighter. I reach my other hand down to cup my balls the way she did and even though it doesn't feel quite the same, my imagination takes over and it isn't long before I'm coming in warm, salty spurts into the water around me. I only hope she didn't overhear my strangled cry as I came; her name had fallen from my lips before I could help myself.

Dried and dressed, I head into the lounge. Nye is sitting in the wingback chair with her feet tucked beneath her. She's subconsciously twirling her hair around her hand. I feel a sharp pang in my heart as I watch her quietly.

Why has no other woman ever captivated me the way Aneurin Mackenzie does? What makes her special enough to catch my attention and keep it for more than one night? Why is it that even when I'm not with her, I'm constantly thinking about her, wondering what she's doing, how she's feeling. And when I am with her, I'm not merely thinking of her in a sexual way, I find myself caring about her, wanting to know the small stuff like how her day was. Before, I would have said that way of thinking was mundane. I would never have sweat the small stuff with the women I hooked up with. What an asshole. Or at least I *used* to be.

Chapter Fourteen

Nye

After spending the day with Preston, I am beginning to think that I might never look at a man in the same way again.

Preston isn't the arrogant jerk I thought he was for so long. He's actually a very interesting, smart, thoughtful, caring man. And, oh man, is he ever an amazing lover. He makes me feel sensations I had long since forgotten it was possible to feel, in fact, the more I think about it, I'm not sure I've ever felt that way. He spent hours last night making me feel desired, sexy, incredible. He looked at me like I was the only woman on the planet.

He's got so much going for him. He's not just rich, he's also talented and intellectual. I know I've said no for so long, but he's going to go over the paperwork for me to sign tomorrow. I'm finally allowing him to help me with *Style in Snowflake.* We spent some time talking about it today and he told me that with the reach of social media advertising as well as paying for adverts in the tabloids in the neighboring towns, I could bring more business to my store and, in turn, maybe to the whole town.

Preston only deals with the business side of things, the paperwork and stuff, but he's getting someone he's worked with before to design a website to bring *Style in Snowflake* to the center of attention. He doesn't only want me to succeed because he likes me or wants to get into my pants—he doesn't need to impress me with grand gestures for that to happen—he wants to help because he knows it will be good for me.

I was too pigheaded and bullish to listen when he came waltzing in wearing his size twelves, stomping all over my once flourishing hometown. Sure, he'd made a lot of improvements and brought new business to town, as well as bringing some of the old businesses back, but *Style in Snowflake* has always been *my* baby and I wanted it to succeed under my leadership. I didn't want to accept the help of anyone else, not just Preston. But I'd taken it out on him and for that, my business didn't suffer, but it didn't flourish either. I'm hoping that's all about to change. I can't wait to embrace the changes and allow someone to help guide the way. The operative word being *help*. I won't allow anyone to take over, but if I'm destined to be a success, I have to eat my own words and allow Preston to do what he promised.

Last night plays on a loop in my head as I get ready to go out with Paisley. There's a music festival over in Blue Ridge she wants to check out. I can't say I've ever heard of most of the bands, but I know there's a tribute act doing songs from some of my favorite artists. It might be as close as I ever get to hearing their music live, so when Paisley called me this morning to see if I was up for it, I found myself agreeing.

Looking at myself in the full-length mirror, I check out the flowy skirt I have chosen to pair with my cowboy boots. It's a modest length but made from a floaty material that looks almost see-through. When I found it at the warehouse, I knew I had to purchase one for myself, even if not for the store. I've chosen to team it up with a black vest top with a checked shirt, unbuttoned but knotted at the waist.

My hair is loose but curled, my makeup is minimal but with a rose red lipstick. I almost wish Preston was coming with us—and not just to prove I own cowboy boots, as I'd told him—but it's just me and Paisley for once. We haven't hung out so much since she started seeing Jack. He seems like a good guy and by the looks of it, he's treating my best friend like the queen I know she is.

Paisley rings the doorbell at six-thirty on the dot. I open the door to see her and Jack standing there. My heart sinks. I thought I was getting my best friend to myself for once. But I plaster a smile on my face and invite them in.

"Mind if I come in too?"

The voice makes me jump out of my skin. I look to see Preston at the side of the house.

"What are you doing here?"

"Jack called and invited me. I guess they want it to be a double date like we're teenagers or something."

"Why were you hiding over there?"

"Because I wanted to surprise you and I'm taller than the two of them, so…"

He pauses and looks at me. His appraisal is slow, taking me in from head to—cowboy boot-clad—toe. The smile that lights his face shows he likes what he sees. All of a sudden, I'm not too mad at Paisley for bringing the boys with her.

"You look…there are no words. This is a different look to what I'm used to on you," he says.

"Thanks. You don't scrub up too badly yourself. I mean, don't get me wrong, I love a man in a three-piece suit—I defy you to find me a woman who doesn't like the suited and booted look—but you look hot in jeans and cowboy boots. Tell me, did you buy them 'vintage' or are they actually worn in?"

"They're worn in, thank you very much. Yes, 'work Preston' walks around in expensive suits, but the other side of me that you don't get to see—he knows how to dress casually and have fun. You'll see."

I would have sworn he didn't even own casual clothes before I'd seen him in a pair of ass-hugging indigo jeans the first time. I'm not silly enough to think he bought some just to impress me or to prove a point, but even if he did, at this moment I wouldn't care. He looks divine and, for once, I am not embarrassed as I take in the sight of him.

***

Alcohol is flowing, there's music in the air and I feel better than I have in a long time. I guess I can get stressed out sometimes, but tonight I've been able to relax. The performances from the tribute artists have been great, the mulled wine I've been drinking has me in the Christmas spirit and the company has been fun too. I was a bit pissed that Paisley had invited the boys, but it turned out I didn't need to be.

The boys have actually given us some time to hang out, just the two of us, while they've gone and done whatever it is boys do for fun these days.

Paisley has been dancing and trying to get me to line dance with her. She's actually a great dancer; she has this vibe about her that's almost ethereal.

The band on stage begin to play "That's My Kind of Night" by Luke Bryan. Paisley grabs my hand, spinning me into a small open space where others are beginning to line dance. I love Luke Bryan. He's so hot and he has an awesome voice. I love a man who can sing or play an instrument, preferably both. It takes me a second or two to get to grips with the dance the others are doing, but I catch on and so does Paisley.

Laughing and shaking loose like this feels so good. The band segues into "Win Life" and the dance we're doing changes to a slightly slower beat.

As we make our way over to the bar, we see the boys heading our way, drinks in hand.

"You ladies look like you need these," Jack says as he hands Paisley and me a bottle of beer.

"You never told me you could dance," Preston says, making me jump when I notice he's closer than I thought.

"I haven't practiced those moves in years, if I'm being honest."

"Well you certainly didn't look out of practice."

"Thank you. But I'm rustier than I used to be. Shall I let you in on a secret? Paisley and I used to take classes when we were kids. She was always better than me, top of the class, but I enjoyed taking part. I felt kind of carefree."

"You both looked great out there. I have two left feet, so I don't dance. But you girls made it look effortless."

"A lot of work goes into making it look 'effortless' Mr. Fitzgerald," Paisley says, air-quoting the word for maximum effect.

"I'm sure it does. That wasn't a remark meant to offend you," he replies, sounding contrite.

"I'm winding you up. Boy, you don't take much, do you? Like an old-fashioned toy with a big key in his back. Easy peasy!"

I can't help the laugh that bubbles out of me, partially spraying beer at the same time.

"Hey, lady! Say it, don't spray it!" she chides me with a smile.

We all crack up at that and I wipe my mouth with the back of my hand.

The music changes to a slower song and Preston takes my hand, guides me to a slightly open space and takes me in his arms.

"I thought you had two left feet?"

"I do, as a rule. But I think anyone can slow dance. It's only moving your feet from side to side."

His arms wrap around me and I rest my head against his chest, feeling his heart as it pounds beneath my cheek.

I sigh a dreamy kind of sigh as I keep my arms around him and my cheek pressed close. Here in his arms, I feel like there's nowhere on earth I'd rather be. But I can't help waiting for the other shoe to drop.

Recently, it feels like we've had a connection. There's an undeniable chemistry there between us, so much so that it's almost tangible. When I'm wrapped in his embrace, I feel like little sparks trail across my skin and my heartbeat has somehow changed. It may sound sappy, but it's almost like my heart beats for him.

But I still can't help but think that our little bubble will burst soon, and reality will come crashing down around my ears. Maybe it's because I don't feel good enough for a man like Preston. Maybe it's because he comes from a wealthy upbringing and is used to a certain way of life and I don't…so I'm wondering how I can fit into his life when I'm nothing like him.

I'm worried about leaving my heart wide open like it is right now. I know he has the power to break me. If he doesn't feel the same, or if he does and then somehow changes his mind, he could shatter my heart into a million tiny shards, each one piercing my skin like a razor blade, leaving me irreparably broken.

But on the other hand, if I close myself off to the possibility of something real with him, I will miss the chance and that would also break my heart. I don't know what to do or how to feel. I'm damned if I do and damned if I don't.

So, I'll stay in my bubble a little longer and wait to see what Preston's next move will be.

I don't know when the song changed, or how long we've been dancing for, but Preston still has me in his embrace and doesn't seem to want to let go.

***

After an awesome night out, Preston drops me back home. He's standing on my doorstep while I try to find my key. His presence makes the hairs on the backs of my arms stand on end. He's electrifying and I can't deny the attraction. I can't seem to tamp it down either. There needs to be a volume remote so that I can dial it down sometimes. I don't always want him to know how he affects me. But I think he will always know, deep down. He seems to have a good intuition as far as I am concerned. I don't know whether that will always be a good thing. Do I want someone who can read me so well?

Once we're inside, I turn in the direction of my kitchen. I retrieve two bottles of beer from the fridge, take the caps off them and hand one to Preston.

I watch him like a hawk as he takes a long, slow pull of his drink before his Adam's apple bobs as he swallows. His square jawline is something I can't take my eyes off. There's just something about a man with good bone structure that is highly appealing.

He catches me watching him and I turn my head, embarrassed. I feel the warm blush creep across my chest and mentally kick myself for being so obvious in my appreciation of him.

"Nye," he whispers as he walks towards me. "Look at me. Please?"

I look up and see a hunger in his eyes. It's intense enough for me to sense it in the air.

Suddenly, his lips slant over mine. They're warm and inviting and his tongue seeks entry to my mouth. His kiss is hot, demanding and impatient, like he can't get enough of me fast enough.

I feel his hand pull my hair back off my shoulders and he holds it back as his lips leave mine and trail hot kisses down my neck to the hollow of my throat.

My breathing is heavy and my body feels alive with his touch as his free hand slips underneath my vest top. His hand splays across my stomach momentarily before wandering up and cupping my breast. His thumb brushes across my nipple over the material of my bra, making me gasp. My back arches me towards him involuntarily. We're standing so close that nothing could come between us. My entire body feels heavy with want, need, lust…and maybe something more. Something inexplicable at this point. Everything is tangled up in knots, twisted in such a way I can't see where it starts and ends.

"Nye, I…you…," he sputters, trying to form a coherent sentence.

I reach for the buttons of his black shirt, fumbling to slip them through the holes. Once they are undone, I slip his shirt down his shoulders and he discards it on the kitchen island behind him.

My hands glide over the firm ridges of his body, my nails digging in when he pulls me closer. Preston turns us around, so my back is to the island and he is standing between my legs. He nudges them further apart, lifts me and perches me on the edge of the granite worktop.

Warmth pools in my abdomen as he kisses me, his tongue dancing with mine.

No words need to be exchanged as he undoes the knot at the front of my shirt and slips it down my arms. Then he reaches for the hem of my vest and breaks our kiss momentarily as he pulls it up over my head. Within seconds, his lips claim mine again in a searing kiss, a kiss that burns so bright I'm sure we're about to combust.

I slip the straps of my bra from my arms and toss it behind me in the direction of his shirt, then pull him closer to me, wanting—no, needing—the feel of his flesh against mine. Our chests are pressed together, our breathing heavy. He rains kisses down on me, down to the hollow of my throat, then to the swell of my breasts as he cups them in his hands and brushes the tips of his thumbs over them.

Small moans slip from my mouth as he sucks one nipple gently into his mouth, licking, sucking and nipping it gently before moving to pay the same attention to the other one.

I dig my heels into his firm ass as my legs cling tightly around his waist. I can feel his hard length through the material of my panties, my skirt hitched up around my waist to keep it out of the way. I reach a hand between us and stroke the length of him from base to tip over the top of his jeans. The throaty moan that leaves him is music to my ears.

I undo the button of his jeans, then his zipper, then slide my hand down and cup him in my palm. His breath hitches in his throat, so I slip my hand underneath the material of his boxer shorts. His hands brace against the kitchen island on either side of me as I stroke him. His breathing is labored and he almost growls in my ear.

Growing in confidence, I slide his jeans and boxers down from his waist. I push the material to his knees and his cock springs free, hard and glistening with pre-cum on the tip.

My tongue darts out to wet my lips and I look up at Preston. His eyes are like magnets, drawing me in. I'm momentarily lost in his gaze, both our bodies motionless, suspended in time.

"Nye…not here…" he whispers, breaking the spell.

I nod my agreement that this isn't the perfect place for this. I don't want a quick fumble on the kitchen island. I want us to be able to take our time to enjoy each other.

He pulls his jeans back up slightly, then lifts me as though I weigh no more than a feather. My legs cling tightly around his waist as he strides to the bottom of my stairs and carries me up to my room.

When we reach my door, I push it wide open and he strides through and places me carefully on the bed.

His eyes search mine and he must find whatever he seeks because he lifts me to slip my skirt from me. Pulling the material of my panties with it, he leaves me lying bare.

Preston stands over me and looks me over from head to toe, his appraisal slow and purposeful—whilst also being an agonizing wait for me. My body misses his touch, though it's only taken away briefly. But brief as it is, there's a longing in me.

I cry out as Preston lowers himself to his knees and circles my clit with his tongue. My hands grip the sheets and my back arches off the bed. He dominates me masterfully and I am at his mercy. The warmth pools in my abdomen again and my legs begin to quiver. My heart beats out a staccato rhythm, trying to break free from its restraints. A delicious shiver runs through me as I cry out my release.

***

Waking in Preston's embrace is something I could get used to. He's intoxicating, something I could drown in easily. I could lose myself in him forever, but that's also what scares me. I've been burned before; relationships have come and gone, some hurting more than others. I'm holding myself back for fear of being truly broken by this man. He holds the power to wreck me even if he doesn't know it yet.

Feeling him stir behind me, I turn in his arms and smile as he opens his eyes. They're like liquid pools of chocolate this morning, though they looked more like molten lava last night as he made love to me over and over again.

We'd fallen asleep together after the first time, my head on his chest as it rose and fell, lulling me into slumber. But then he'd woken when I started to kiss his chest, his abs and then lower. I'd held on as the earth shattered around me and I'd cried out into the night like a wild animal.

"Morning sunshine," he whispers as he props himself up on the pillow next to me.

"Morning."

I reach out and trace a hand over the feather tattoo he has going over the right side of his chest. It's the only tattoo he has and it's beautiful, delicate and intricate, and seems to hold a meaning I'm unable to grasp. The black ink is highlighted by white ink that make it stand out against his tanned skin.

"You didn't have this…before," I say as I trace the outline.

"It's new, still healing."

"Does it mean something?"

"Strength, courage, bravery…the feather can mean different things to different people."

I'm guessing by that answer he doesn't want to tell me what it means to him. I look at it more closely and see that it is indeed still healing. I find myself hoping I didn't hurt him last night because I see fingernail marks not too far from the tip of the feather.

"It's beautiful."

It's breathtaking, really.

"Thank you, I designed it myself."

"You draw?"

Another side of Preston I didn't know about sooner.

"A little. Mainly as a way of unwinding. I used to think I wanted to be an architect or something like that. I wanted to put my art to good use. But my father dying put paid to that idea because it meant I had to take over the Fitzgerald family business in the event of my grandfather's death."

"You're very talented."

I admire the ink from a whole new perspective, appreciating the fact that he drew it himself.

"It's only a feather. If you're impressed by that, you should see my old portfolio."

"You should show me sometime. Did you do the blueprints and stuff when you helped the businesses here in Snowflake?"

"No. Unfortunately, I don't have that kind of time anymore. My job is pretty full on. I mean, business ebbs and flows, but when it's busy, it really does get busy and I don't have 'spare' time to doodle."

I'm amazed to hear him refer to his drawing as doodling, but I feel it's not a subject I should push, so instead I lean up and place a chaste kiss on his lips.

As I attempt to withdraw and get out of bed, strong arms wrap around me and keep me firmly in place and his tongue duels with mine for dominance over a breathtaking, dizzying kiss.

Chapter Fifteen

Preston

Being back in the office feels like torture. I can't shake the feelings that surrounded me when I was with Nye. I'm back in work so I should be all business. But I'm not. I'm sitting and doodling on a piece of paper as Cordelia drones on about something or other. I tuned out as soon as she opened her mouth, more or less.

Closing my eyes for a moment, I picture Nye: gorgeous emerald eyes sparkling with amusement, full pink lips, her brown hair falling down over her bare breasts…

I can still feel her beneath my fingertips, her soft, supple skin. The hairs on the back of my neck rise as I recall the breathtaking kiss I left her with this morning. I hadn't got any meetings until this afternoon, so I'd gone home and had a shower, even though I was reluctant to leave her. Then I'd made my way into work, but it felt like it was all done on autopilot.

Cordelia clearing her throat brings me back to my office. I open my eyes and see a flicker of something in her eyes. Resentment? Jealousy? I can't pin it down.

"Am I keeping you from something, Preston?" she seethes as she turns her back on me and walks over to my liquor cabinet.

"Sorry, I was lost in a world of my own there. Late night, didn't sleep well."

"Working late?" she asks as she pours a measure of my Macallan and passes it to me.

"I…umm…" I don't really want to tell her about Nye because it's none of her business, but Cordelia is like a dog with a bone. "No, I was with someone."

I sip my drink and relish the warmth as it goes down.

"Ah. A hook-up keeps you up late, then you can't concentrate the next day? I must say, that's not like you, Preston. You're more professional than to let your…umm…sex life impede on your real life."

"It wasn't like that. Really Cordelia, it's none of your business anyway."

"It is when it interferes with making money, Preston. When you're not listening to me go over an important business deal. A potentially very lucrative one, may I add."

"We don't have any deals to push through, Cordelia. What are you on about?"

She's acting like I'm a child she can chastise or put on the naughty step. She seems to forget this is my company; she only works here. And the only reason she still stayed on here after we split up was because I couldn't sack her just for being my ex. If I had my way, she'd leave and never look back. I'm looking forward to her maternity leave. Who knows, maybe when she has the baby, she'll decide she doesn't want to come back to work. A boy can but dream!

***

The rest of the day went by in slow motion. I had some paperwork to do and a proposal to look through. Nothing that couldn't have waited. I *could* have spent the day in bed with Nye. She could have told Paisley she wasn't going in. But there's no point wallowing in what I *could* have been doing.

I sit with a glass of Macallan in my hand, looking out of the window. I wish Nye was here. I feel like a lovestruck teenager. I'm constantly thinking of her. Why can't I just tell the girl how I really feel?

Moving over to my favorite wingback chair, I pick up my dog-eared, well-loved, re-read tons of times, copy of *Desperation*, a Stephen King novel, and hope to lose myself for a while, distracting myself from the real world.

Just as I'm getting into the story, Cordelia texts, saying she's had some paperwork drawn up and left in my office for me to go over tomorrow. I was the last one in the office today, so I guess she must have gone back after I left. She's a workaholic, that girl.

Deciding on an early night, I turn the lights out and head for the stairs. As I look back over my shoulder, I see the lights twinkling on the tree that Nye helped me pick out and decorate. A smile forms on my face and I turn back and head for my room.

***

I'm up at the ass-crack of dawn, dressed in running gear, with sweat pouring out of me. A five-mile run was just what the doctor ordered. I had my music on my iPod, and my feet pounded the pavement. Time for a quick shower before heading into work.

Fully suited and booted and ready for the day ahead, I take one last look in the mirror before heading out the door.

I have meetings back to back, a chockablock day in store. I don't know about Christmas being "the most wonderful time of the year", but it sure is the busiest.

After a meeting with the board, I go back to my office to check for any messages before heading into another meeting. This one is due to be the most boring; it's with the accountants to talk over financial crap. That's the thing I hate about running the family business instead of working for someone else or being an architect as I wanted. I wouldn't have had to worry about money affairs then.

Taking a quick look at the paperwork Cordelia left on my desk, I see it's the social media and website stuff for *Style in Snowflake*. I'll have to call Nye to discuss it after I've met with the accountants.

I make myself a cup of coffee and head back into the boardroom. Bang goes the rest of my day.

Chapter Sixteen

Nye

Preston called a little while ago, so I'm driving over to his office to sign the paperwork for the help he's giving me with the store.

He contracted the website design out and wants me to come and take a look to see if I like it before hitting publish.

There are also some social media adverts he wants my approval on. Apparently, I should expect business to boom after they go live.

The store is ready for Christmas, just like most of the town. Paisley is looking after the place while I do the paperwork with Preston and I plan on asking him today to help me draw up the paperwork for Paisley to be my business partner instead of just my assistant.

I pull into the parking space and look up at the building in front of me. It's imposing, yet impressive. It reeks of money. It's okay if you like that kind of thing, but, honestly, I've never been a materialistic girl; money doesn't really matter to me beyond paying the bills each month. Another reason I'm not good enough for Preston in the long run. I don't earn anywhere near as much money as he does. He's used to the finer things in life like champagne and caviar and all the things people with money enjoy. I'm used to being a jeans and t-shirt kind of girl. He's used to being suited, booted and in charge. Although, the "in charge" thing is something I could come to appreciate.

Pulling my mind out of the gutter, I enter the building. Again, I'm sitting in the gorgeous reception area waiting for him to call me through. I enjoy the luxury of the leather chair and the espresso the receptionist made for me while I wait.

I look up to see Preston in a dark grey, three-piece suit. It's paired with a crisp white shirt and a black tie. His tiepin looks like a real diamond—and with his money, it probably is—and his shoes are so well polished, I could see my face in them.

Taking in his chiseled jawline and his gorgeous warm brown eyes, my heart beats a little harder in my chest. He looks so handsome. Beyond handsome really, but I'm out of descriptive words.

As he takes my hand and helps me stand, I take in a deep breath, drawing the scent of sandalwood into my lungs and storing it in my memory.

"Good afternoon, Nye. It's nice to see you. If you'll follow me," he says in a clipped kind of way.

His tone isn't warm and friendly; it isn't the Preston I've come to know.

Following him into his office, I take in the sight of his delectable ass. I feel a little warm as I remember what it looks like underneath the suit.

Seeing Cordelia sat in his office, I try to smile but it doesn't feel genuine and she can probably tell. I don't know what it is, but I just don't like the woman. I barely know her, but she gets under my skin and I don't like the feeling.

"Aneurin," she greets me with a smile that's as fake as mine.

She stretches out her perfectly manicured hand and I feel a little self-conscious as I take it in mine, noticing my own chipped nail varnish. I keep meaning to go and get my typical Christmas-style manicure with little Santa hats and gems on them, but work is busy. And when I haven't been at work, I've been with Preston.

I feel him standing close behind me, so close I can feel his warmth seeping from his body to mine. I wish we had the room to ourselves.

Sitting in the chair Preston holds out for me, I see papers spread all over his desk. Organized chaos? Doesn't seem like his style, but what do I know?!

We go over the social media ads and Cordelia taps away on her phone with a clickety-clacking sound that drives me bonkers. Is she even listening? Maybe she's making notes on what I have to say, or maybe she's typing a status out saying how much she hates being trapped in here with me. That's what I'd probably be doing if the shoe was on the other foot.

Once I've approved the ads, I spy blueprints with the name of the store on the top. Cordelia has gone to make a coffee, so it's just me and Preston, but he doesn't look like he's letting his guard down. He smiles at me, but his usual warmth is lacking. Maybe this is just the work side of him and he's compartmentalizing, keeping his love life separate.

His love life? Is that what it is?

I turn back to the blueprints, look at the layout and notice it doesn't look much like my store. Does Preston expect me to change the store to fit a certain kind of image? I don't think I like that idea much. This is my business, not his. And whilst he may have a head for business, I actually only agreed to let him help me with a website and social media. Why would he need blueprints for that?

"Preston, what is this?" I ask, gesturing to the paper on his desk.

He clears his throat and leans over me to look where I'm pointing.

"I don't know. Cordelia brought all the paperwork in here."

"It looks oddly like blueprints for *Style in Snowflake,* but it looks nothing like the layout for my store. We didn't discuss changing anything and I don't appreciate the idea of someone trying to strong-arm me into doing something."

"I'm not trying to strong-arm anyone into anything, Aneurin. You know me, I wouldn't do that."

He picks the blueprints up and looks them over.

"I didn't ask Cordelia to do this. I swear. I'll have words with her, tear this up and forget it existed. I'm sorry, Nye."

Cordelia walks back into the room and must sense the hostility coming off me in waves. Her smile is awkward and forced.

"What is this?" Preston asks, directing her attention to the paper he's holding.

"The blueprints for the new store. The layout is only rough, we can change anything Aneurin isn't happy with, of course."

"Wait, hold on a minute. Did you just say *new* store? What the hell does that mean?"

I'm trying to hold back the venom lacing my words, but it's difficult to bite my tongue.

"Yes, the new store. The one we're here to discuss. Is there a problem?"

"We're not here to discuss a *new* store. We're only here to discuss a website for my store and the social media adverts. Other than that, my business is just that... *mine.*"

"Darling, nobody said it wasn't yours. We're just here to discuss the layout for the new store. I'm sorry, I don't get what the problem is.

You're moving to a new location; hence you need blueprints for a new layout for the builders."

"What?" I screech, quickly losing hold of my composure.

I look to Preston and see his eyes look dark. Anger rolls off him in waves. It's palpable and I'm not sure who it's directed at.

"Darling..."

"Don't darling me. I'm not your darling. I'm not anybody's darling. Get that straight right now," I seethe as I stand. "I don't care what you have to say, but you'd better listen to me. I am *not* moving my store—not now, not *ever*. I never agreed to any of this. I don't know where you even got the idea I would be willing to relocate. I don't know if there's actually a brain in your head, or whether there's a wide open space. But get this through your thick skull—you are not going to strong-arm me into moving. You might be used to men falling at your feet and giving you what you want, but I won't be following in their footsteps."

"Oh, I'm sorry, darling." She emphasizes the word to annoy me. "I'm sorry to tell you, but you've already signed the paperwork."

She points to a contract on the desk. I grab it and read it over. I signed some paperwork, thinking it was for the work they were doing for me. I turn over to the next page and see that it looks like she fooled me into signing something that gave her—the Fitzgerald company—the chance to relocate my store.

Unable to stay here a moment longer, I grab my bag and storm from the room.

"You'll be hearing from my lawyer," I shout back over my shoulder. "Don't think you've heard the last of this, Preston Fitzgerald."

I don't have a lawyer, but I damn well need to find one now. How could I be so stupid as to only read the front page and sign on the dotted line? I signed twice. I didn't realize they were separate contracts. Why would they want to fool me like that? How could Preston do that to me?

Is this why he's been intimate with me, just to fool me into signing something? I really thought we might have had something. We could have had something real. But that was all in my head. All that was in his was tricking me, making me believe he could feel the same.

What I'm trying but failing to understand is why they want to relocate the store. What do they gain from it? I don't know, but I'm damn sure going to find out.

I slip my phone out of my pocket, text Paisley and tell her I'm not feeling well. She tells me she'll take care of the store for the day. I start the engine and drive. I don't know or care where I'm going, I just want to get away from here.

***

Twenty missed calls, fifteen new text messages, three new voicemails… I can't be bothered to listen to or read anything that bastard has to say. I delete them without care.

Betrayal stings as I wipe the tears from my eyes. I thought Preston really liked me. I should have known that a girl like me wasn't made for a man like him. He has expensive tastes, even down to the damn pen I signed his contracts with. I somehow came home with it by accident and, after sitting and staring at it for a while, a quick Google search told me that it's a Mont Blanc limited edition "Leonardo" fountain pen. Over two and a half grand's worth of pen. What the ever-loving hell? Who in their right mind spends that much on a pen?

My phone ringing interrupts my thoughts. I look at the screen and see Preston's face in a photo I took of him. He looks so handsome, a candid shot he didn't know I was taking.

I decline the call, sending him to voicemail. Another message I won't listen to.

I pull up his number and block him. Thank goodness for the iPhone's blocking option.

That ought to get me some peace and quiet.

I scrub my eyes with the heels of my hands and let out a shaky breath. There is another way of looking at this, I guess; I had a lucky escape. I found out what kind of person he was before giving him my heart. Still, my heart feels heavy. A dull, physical ache in my chest lingers.

A knock at the door startles me and I make my way wearily to look through the peephole to see who it is.

The sight of Paisley's blonde hair and blue eyes make me smile, the first on my face for hours.

I open the door and she greets me with a grin, brandishing a bottle of wine my way. I told her I was ill, but it looks like she didn't buy my story.

"You okay babe?" she asks as she looks me up and down.

"Yeah." My voice comes out a little croaky.

I clear my throat and move aside to let her in.

Taking stock of the state of the lounge, Paisley goes into the kitchen and walks back with two wine glasses. She fills one and hands it to me.

"Want to talk about it?" she asks as she perches on the couch.

"Not really."

I sit and take a large gulp of my wine.

"But you're going to anyway."

Looking at her, I see the only person I know who has never stabbed me in the back.

"I've made a big mistake. I signed some paperwork and fucked up."

Paisley tops up my wine glass and sits back, waiting for me to explain.

I give her the short version of the story and she looks at me with sympathy in her eyes. I swallow, my throat dry. I don't know what to do. I did a Google search for lawyers over in Blue Ridge as we don't have one here in Snowflake. I called and made an appointment with one and now Paisley has agreed to come with me for support.

"For what it's worth, babe, you are more than deserving of a man like Preston. It's him who's turned out to be unworthy of you."

"I don't understand why he'd do this to me. I mean, why not just be honest from the start, you know?! Why go through the motions of making me think we have something worth pursuing, all to get me to sign the paperwork? Why not just talk to me about relocating? I could have saved him time and me a ton of heartache by just saying no."

"Maybe he thought that by lulling you into a false sense of security, maybe even love, you'd be more open to signing?"

"But then why hide the paperwork? Why trick me into signing it instead of showing it to me?"

"That's a good point. Why the secrecy? The trickery?"

"No offense, Pais, but my head is mush. Mind if I get an early night and we can go over things tomorrow? I'll come back to it with fresher eyes and see if that helps me gain perspective."

Paisley stands and pulls me up with her. She wraps her arms around me and I feel lighter for having shared my burden with my best friend. I may not be able to join the dots and see the bigger picture yet, but Paisley being here has made me feel better.

I walk her to the door and we say our goodbyes. I watch as she gets in her car and drives away. I'm glad she only had one small glass of wine, else I wouldn't have felt comfortable letting her drive.

I close the door and rest my back against it. I'm wiped out, emotionally and physically tired. Maybe a good night's sleep will help me see things more clearly.

A sudden knock at the door has me jumping a mile in the air. I open it, assuming Paisley forgot something.

"Nye…could we please talk?"

I go to slam the door in Preston's handsome but irritating face, but he jams his foot in the way.

His palm comes up against the door and pushes it open. As tired as I am, he doesn't meet much resistance.

"Preston, please, just go away. Did you not get the message?"

"Nye, you ignored all my calls, didn't return my texts, and then imagine my surprise as I try to call you and get nothing. The phone didn't ring, just went right to voicemail. I thought for a minute you might have turned your phone off, but then Cordelia said it was more likely you had blocked me."

"Oh, Cordelia said. Then it must be true. Why are you even trying to get me to talk to you? Surely Cordelia has all the answers!"

He rolls his eyes at the heavy sarcasm lacing my voice.

"Nye, please—"

"You have nothing to say that I want to hear. Just get lost, Preston. You did this. You made me like you. Made me fall for you. Took my heart and ripped it to shreds. Why? All so you could get me to move my store. But I don't even get why. What does it matter to you where my store is located? You know what, I don't want to know. You can tell my lawyer. Now go the hell away."

"I didn't do any of that, Nye. It was Cordelia. That paperwork was as much a shock to me as it was to you. Hold on, what did you just say? I made you *fall* for me?"

I remain stoic and silent as he looks me over from head to toe, taking in my crumpled state.

"Nye … please answer me. I made you fall for me?"

His voice drips with pain. But how can he be in pain here? He's hurt me, not the other way around.

"That's not what's important here, Preston. You know, that stupid nickname you have for yourself, it's pretty fitting. You are a wolf. A wolf in sheep's clothing."

"More like a lamb to the slaughter right now, Aneurin. You're breaking my heart."

I turn and walk away from him. I'm so done with this conversation. "Aneurin, I … I love you."

I spin around so fast I nearly lose my balance. What did he just say?

Strong arms wrap around me and warm lips meld with mine. His tongue seeks access to my mouth and I allow him to deepen the kiss. His chest rises and falls rapidly, his breathing uneven as he pours unspoken words into his kiss.

Why does it feel so right to be in his arms after what's happened? I need my head reading. Who knows, maybe I'll see a shrink about this whole mess.

"I'm sorry," he whispers as he breaks the kiss.

"I need to know what you meant, Preston. What did Cordelia do?"

He told me he loved me and all I can think about is the future of my store. Maybe I am nuts. Preston Fitzgerald declared his love for me and I'm ignoring the pang in my chest. I can't let myself believe it isn't another trick designed to fool me.

"She's been sacked, and the paperwork has been torn up. *Style in Snowflake* is staying right where it is. Truth be told, I've wanted her out of the business since we split up, but I didn't have a reason. Now I have gross misconduct."

He takes my hand in his, leads me to the lounge and we sit on the couch.

Giving me the long and short of it, Preston explains how Cordelia saw an opening to move my store and she took it. She had the blueprints drawn up and the contract too. She wanted me out of Snowflake and out of Preston's life and that was the best way she could figure how. You have to give the girl props for being smart enough to do all that.

Preston confronted her after I left and wouldn't back down until he got answers. She confessed that she'd done it because she was jealous. She wanted Preston to look at her the way she'd seen him look at me.

"There's something else," he says, sounding resigned and deflated. "She's not pregnant. She never was. Not even the first time."

His voice is pained, and I hear it break as he tries to explain how they never lost a baby. He grieved for a baby that never even existed.

What kind of sick person invents a baby? Cordelia Madison needs her head read. The absolute bitch. How—just how—could she do that to Preston?

Wrapping my arms around him, I feel him sag against my chest.

His head rests in the crook of my neck and I stroke his hair, whispering meaningless words to soothe him.

As he pulls himself together, Preston leans away from me and takes my chin in his hand.

"I meant what I said, Aneurin Mackenzie. I love you. I. Love. You."

Each word he punctuates makes me sure I've never known love before. I thought I did, but if what I feel for Preston is love, then no, I've never experienced anything like it in my life.

"I love you too, Preston. I'm sorry I—"

He silences me with a soul-searing kiss. Apologies can wait. Nothing matters in this moment except the love I feel coursing through my veins. I couldn't admit it before, but now that I can…now I can embrace the feeling.

Chapter Seventeen

Preston

I wake up in a familiar room, one that isn't my own. I look down and see brown hair splayed across my chest. Inhaling the intoxicating scent of her, I stroke my hand down the smooth skin of her back. She stirs at my touch and turns to face me.

"Good morning," I say as I lean down to claim her lips.

"It is now," she replies as she pulls back, breathless.

"About last night—"

She silences me with a kiss that makes my cock twitch. My heart feels full as I know that she requites the love I feel for her. I almost pinch myself to see if this is all a dream, but a hand reaches down and strokes the length of my cock and confirms I am indeed awake.

I turn her over onto her back, my arms braced on either side of her head. I lean down and claim her lips in a hungry kiss. My cock hardens as she writhes against me. I align my body with hers and sink slowly into her. Once our bodies are as close as we can get, I start to rock, a slow rhythm.

Searching for more, Nye bucks her hips against me, teasing me, taunting me. I don't think I could ever get enough of this. Of her.

Realization had dawned on me as Cordelia confessed what she had done out of jealousy to tear us apart. Really, I'd known I was in love with Nye before then, but it took that moment to make it truly sink in.

***

"I don't know what you want me to say, Preston. I did this for us," Cordelia had seethed.

Her blood pressure is sure to be through the roof and that can't be good for her or her baby, but she wouldn't listen when I tried to calm her down.

Anything I say makes her worse. Her outbursts aren't really making any sense. What exactly does she think she was doing for "us'?

"What do you even mean, Cordelia? What have you done?"

"I decided we'd be better off and stand a better chance at getting back together if she was no longer in the picture. I could have won you back if it wasn't for her digging her claws in."

"What?" I shout as my blood begins to boil with rage. *She tried to get Nye out of town so that she could have me to herself?*

"You know it's always been me and you, Preston. Always."

"No, Cordelia. We don't work together. We never did, and we never will. There are so many reasons, but this, you trying to control my life, that is one of them."

"You didn't know what you wanted. But I always knew. It was meant to be you and me forever."

"But it wasn't and that had nothing to do with Nye. I hadn't even met her then. Now you're telling me that you made her sign a contract to get her out of my life? How dare you! I knew you were willing to stoop to many levels, Cordelia, but not this. You tricked her. You didn't discuss it with me."

"Because you wouldn't have made her leave. You would have turned against me."

"And what would you have said when it all happened? How would you have explained it to me?"

"I would have told the truth. Sometimes it's better to seek forgiveness than to ask permission. So, I had the contract drawn up."

"This contract?" I ask, the anger rolling off me in waves.

I hold the contract aloft between both hands. The air in the room is silent, but the tension is so thick you could cut it with a knife. The sound of the paper tearing in half is all that can be heard. It's almost deafening.

"Preston!" she cries out, but it's too late. What's done is done.

I tear the paper again and then push each piece through my shredder for good measure.

"I won't let you do that to her, Cordelia. And, as for the fact that you did all this without my express consent, I can only construe it as gross misconduct. Anything like this needs to go through me as CEO. You had no right to do what you did, even if you hadn't actually tricked her. You had no right getting the company lawyer to draw those papers up. It's done. You're done. I'm sorry Cordelia, you leave me no choice but to fire you."

"Fire me? What the—" she sputters.

I can see the rage in her eyes as she looks at me in shock.

"I'm going to have to ask you to leave your building pass with the receptionist. Please clear your desk and don't come back."

I turn my back on her, walk to the window and look out over the rainy sky. I need to get Nye to hear me out. I need her to know this wasn't me. Will she listen to me? I can only hope.

"I love you, Preston. That's why I did this."

"You love me? This isn't love, it's control and manipulation. And what about the father of your baby? Won't he have something to say about this? You do remember him, right? His name is Blake in case you had forgotten."

"There is no baby, Preston. There never was."

My head whips round in shock. I look at her and she shrugs.

"I invented it. I thought it would make you jealous."

She doesn't even have the decency to look the least bit contrite.

"Are you on drugs? Women don't invent babies. And the fact that you did— why would you do that? You say you wanted me to be jealous, but how would carrying another man's baby win me back?"

"I admit, I didn't think it through fully before that lie slipped from my mouth. I just wanted you back. I thought the baby lie might bring us closer together because of when I told you we were pregnant and that I'd lost it. You were a mess over that baby."

"So, you invent a baby? You think I'd want to bring up another man's baby with you? It makes no sense!"

"It wouldn't be the first time," she mutters under her breath.

Had I not been listening so carefully, I may have missed it.

"You mean you've done this to someone else?"

Shock registers on her face as it begins to dawn on her what she actually said. Maybe she hadn't meant to say it out loud.

"No."

I look at Cordelia Madison, a woman who is usually so together. At this moment, she's falling apart and that isn't something I've ever seen happen to her.

On one hand, I've sacked her, and I just want her out of the building and out of my life. On the other hand, this is a woman I almost had a child with. I grieved the loss of our baby. I may not have been head over heels in love with Cordelia the way I am with Nye, but that baby meant something to me.

"Cordelia, we go way back. You can be honest with me."

"I've never been pregnant, Preston. I thought you were going to leave me, so I blurted out the first thing that came to mind."

"You tricked me into believing you were having a baby?"

I run my fingers through my hair as I pace the floor of my office.

"How could you?" I roar, making her shrink in on herself.

"I ... I was young and stupid."

"But you're not young and stupid now, Cordelia, and you've invented a second baby. I can't believe you let me grieve for the loss of a baby that was never even conceived. You're a lying, deceitful, manipulative bitch. Pack up your desk. Get out of my building and out of my life. If I EVER see you again, it will be too soon!"

"I faked losing the baby because I could see you didn't really love me. It was my way of letting you out of the relationship."

"What would you have done when you didn't gain weight? When we didn't attend scans? When your due date came and there was no baby?" I pause to take a deep breath, "Hang on, we went to a scan. WE actually went to a scan and they told us our baby had died. If you weren't pregnant, then what was that all about?"

She looks at me and I see pity flash in her eyes.

"It was all just a lie, Preston. I'm sorry. I'm so very sorry. I booked a scan, but when the sonographer looked, she said there was no baby. Nobody actually mentioned the word miscarriage. You assumed, and I let you believe it. But there had never been a baby to begin with."

She looks crestfallen, which is exactly how I feel. How could she have ever done this? It's one thing to invent a baby, but to take me to a scan, knowing there wasn't a baby to begin with? That's another level of screwed up.

"What happened the next day when you had to go to hospital?"

"I didn't really have an appointment."

"So, what the hell did you do that day when you told me you were so heartbroken, and you needed to go alone? I begged you to let me go with you. Now I know why you wouldn't let me. What the hell, Cordelia? In fact, no, you know what, I don't need to know. Now GET THE FUCK OUT OF HERE!"

She turns and leaves my office. I sink down into my chair and put my head in my hands. Why would she do that? She's in need of a psychiatrist. And I'm in need of a drink. Then I need to go and grovel to Nye to hear me out.

***

The memory of the argument with Cordelia is still fresh in my memory, but I need to move on. I need to put the past aside and concentrate on the future.

I lie awake next to Nye, watching her sleep soundly. Propping my head up on my hand, I lie on my side, just looking at her. She's beautiful in her slumber. But then she's beautiful at all times, even when she's angry.

Tonight, she heard me out, even though I thought she wasn't going to. She's just as beautiful on the inside as she is on the outside.

I can't believe she loves me. What have I done to deserve the love of such an amazing woman? I am genuinely besotted by her, deeply in love with her and I'm shit scared of that if I'm being honest. I've never been in love, never. I don't know what happened to the cold, unloving guy I used to be. No, scrap that, I know exactly what happened to him—Aneurin Mackenzie walked into his life.

She rolls onto her side, so I snuggle up behind her, wrap my arm around her waist and lie my head on the pillow. I want to go to sleep and wake up next to her for the rest of my life. The old me would have been scared by that kind of thought. In fact, he never would have thought like that at all. But now? Now I know what I want, and I just have to prove to Nye that she can trust me and that I am worthy of her love. I'll never hurt her. She did the impossible; she scaled the walls around my heart and brought them down, brick by brick at first, and then all at once the walls collapsed.

***

I wake up to see a sleeping Nye in my arms and can't stop the smile that spreads across my face. I want to do something special for her, but I don't know what.

I know she loves Christmas and that she embraces the feel-good vibes of the festive season. Can I use that to my advantage?

"I know you're awake. I can feel you moving behind me," she says in a sleepy voice.

"Good morning."

She turns in my arms and looks up at me through her long lashes. My heart skips a beat as she smiles up at me.

"Aneurin, I'm so sorry."

"Shhh!" she says as she puts a finger to my lips.

"But I—" I try to speak around her finger, but she presses it harder against my mouth.

"No. Let's treat today as the first day of our fresh start. We don't need to talk about what's done. None of it can be undone, but it can be forgotten. You tore up the paperwork, you sacked the sneaky, manipulative bitch. You did all you could, and you did that for me. That's worth more than any apology."

I lean down and kiss her soft lips. She gently nips my bottom lip between her teeth and I growl at her playfully.

***

I'm back in the office, the last place I want to be. But I want to make sure Cordelia is gone, along with all trace of her. Plus, the cases she's working on will have to be overseen by somebody else now.

Nye went into work this morning with a smile on her face. Her last words to me were those three words that make my heart beat faster.

I can't believe I've found a good woman to love me for me and not try to change me. Nye isn't interested in my money either. Unlike Cordelia, materialistic things don't matter to Nye.

A smile has taken up permanent residence on my face and, according to Jack, you can hear that smile in my voice. He called when I was in the car on the way here. Initially, he'd phoned to bollock me for hurting Nye, but once I told him it was all sorted, he stopped nagging me.

Deciding to do something frivolous and not work-related, I jump in my car and head towards the shops in the middle of town.

I told Jenny to hold all my calls and rearrange my meetings. It's December fifteenth, meaning there are only ten more days until Christmas. The staff in my office normally work up until the twenty-first and then I work over Christmas Eve, Christmas Day and Boxing Day myself. Business never sleeps. Then when it's New Year, my staff are off and I work New Year's Eve and New Year's Day by myself. The only time I take off is the couple of days between Boxing Day and New Year's Eve.

My staff must think I'm the Grinch who stole Christmas. They work so hard and the only thanks they get for it is extra money in their pay packet. They get a decent Christmas bonus. But I've come to realize that isn't good enough. They need time off with their families.

I haven't told them all yet, but I'm hosting a company Christmas party tomorrow and then they are all going home until January seventh. I want them to have quality time with their loved ones. And of course, they'll still receive their Christmas bonus. A generous amount, at that.

***

Loaded up with bags and boxes, I return to my office and place them all in the corner. I have some calls to make for the catering and to see if I can get some temps from the agency over in Blue Ridge to work the party.

Sometimes it's good to be a Fitzgerald. It gets things done. I don't normally use it to my advantage, but I relent just this once, so I can get things sorted.

I make some calls and arrange everything, then I call Nye and ask if she'll come to the office tonight once everyone has gone home. I'd love her help with the decorating. She has more of an eye for these things than me.

She suggested calling Jack and asking for a hand with the heavier lifting and said she'd ask Paisley to come along too.

I look at all the meetings meant to happen between now and New Year, all the conference calls I'm meant to make and everything my staff are meant to be doing. It takes a while, but I finally manage to postpone everything until after the office reopens. Some of the people I spoke to weren't exactly pleased that they'd have to wait, whereas others were only too happy to be able to give their staff a bit more time off.

The last of my staff leave as Jack is arriving. I hear his car pull up before I see it. He likes to have a car with a lot of horsepower. It's about the only thing that he's splashed out on. He has money, he just chooses to live a simpler life than I do. I have expensive tastes, always have had. But Nye is slowly changing me. Not intentionally, and she probably doesn't even realize she's doing it, but I find myself slowly shedding my flash, cocky persona. I'm not as bothered by labels on things as I used to be.

"What's up buddy? Why am I here when nobody else is?" he greets as he lifts his hand for a fist bump.

"I need your help shifting some heavy stuff around."

"Perfect, just what I need tonight. I was meant to be seeing Paisley. I hope you know you've cost me a date."

"As it happens, Paisley is coming along too. She and Nye should be here any minute."

That puts a smile back on his face. It's the first time I've seen him truly light up when thinking or talking about a woman.

"So, you only want me for my muscles? Nice. I'm not a piece of meat, you know. You can't just objectify me."

"Sorry, bud. I can't help it. You're just so…muscly. So…masculine. Manly."

Jack flashes me a flexed bicep as he laughs at me and shakes his head.

He whips his head around as he hears another car arrive.

Nye's Mercedes pulls up in front of the building. Being gentlemen, we hold their doors open for them and offer a hand to help them from the car.

Nye smiles at me and I take in her Christmassy outfit. She's dressed in green with an elf hat sat askew on her head. She looks so cute. I pull her in for a kiss, but all too soon we're interrupted by Jack clearing his throat. I'd meant the kiss to be brief and sweet, but I guess it got a little more than that. I can't help it. I can't keep my hands to myself when Nye is around, and I want to kiss her all the time. When I'm not kissing her, I'm thinking about kissing her. About tasting that sweet taste that is all Nye.

After a couple of hours of hard work—all done whilst playing Christmas songs from Nye's iPod—we come to a stop. Standing back and looking at everything, I am extremely pleased. It looks like a winter wonderland in here.

"Looking good, Mr. Fitzgerald," Jack says as he sidles up to me.

"I have some waiting staff hired for the day and the caterers were able to fit me in last minute. Thankfully they'd had a cancellation, and being a Fitzgerald helps. I hate using my name to get things done, but when they knew it was me, they bent over backward to accommodate me."

"It sure looks Christmassy in here now," Paisley says as she walks over and puts a piece of tinsel around Jack's neck.

He places a chaste kiss on her lips and smiles down at her as they break apart.

"It's a good job one of us has an eye for decorating," Nye says as she gets down from the top of the ladder.

Her foot catches and almost in slow motion I can see what's going to happen. I rush to her just in time to catch her, my heart pounding in my chest. I should have been holding the ladder for her, I shouldn't have listened when she batted me away saying she'd be fine.

"I told you that you'd end up falling for me," I joke as my heartbeat thuds in my ears.

"Trust you to be totally cheesy!"

She laughs as she looks up at me, but I can see she's still a little shaken, knowing she could have been hurt.

"Are you alright, babe?" Paisley asks over my shoulder.

My heartbeat slowly returns to normal.

"I'm fine. Wolf here caught me."

"Wolf? What the…?"

They both crack up laughing and I hear Jack chuckling behind us. I wish I'd never told her that used to be my nickname. It sounds totally cheesy, but it really is only from the fact that my middle name is Wolfric, and I hate my first name but can't really shorten that without it sounding dumb.

***

The four of us decide to hit Mistletoe & Wine for a few drinks. We're sitting at the bar doing something I didn't think you'd ever catch me dead doing—drinking mulled wine. What the hell am I doing? I'm a whiskey man. Nye is turning me into the kind of man that would do anything she asked. Some might accuse me of being "pussy-whipped" but I prefer to think that I'm just opening up to trying new things.

Jack's busy regaling the girls with stories from our teenage years. He's already told them some pretty embarrassing things, but I find I don't really care right now. I want Nye to know me, all of me—the good, the bad and the ugly. And the embarrassing. I want her to know I have no secrets from her. I've never tried to hide what kind of person I am, and she's never tried to change me. Yet she is changing me slowly. Or, more specifically, her love is changing me, but not in a bad way.

I never thought I'd want to find love. I never saw myself settling down and having children. So why is it that now, all I can imagine is Nye with the perfect baby bump. She'd stand there with that glow about her that pregnant women get, her emerald green eyes sparkling with love and adoration. That mental picture there, that's my whole world.

Chapter Eighteen

Nye

Preston has invited me to his office Christmas party, so I'm busy searching my whole store for something to wear. We do a small line of alternative cocktail dresses. I'm looking for something red and sophisticated, yet a little slinky.

Paisley suddenly whoops and hollers across the other side of the store. I look over to see her holding the most gorgeous red dress.

"Oh my god, it's perfect! It's so you, Nye."

She comes running across the store and brandishes the dress my way. I must agree, it is perfect. It's a deep red, off the shoulder style dress. It cuts off just a little above the knee with lace trim across the hem and the neckline. Elbow length lace sleeves make it look pretty and girly.

I take it from Paisley and walk into one of our dressing rooms. Once it's on and done up, I look at myself in the floor to ceiling mirror. It doesn't show any cleavage, but the lace across the bust looks sexy and understated. It's vintage and very much my style. It cinches me in at the waist and flares out at the knee; I couldn't love this dress more. It gives me a silhouette I'm not ashamed of. I've never been embarrassed about not being stick thin; I've got curves and I'm going to rock them in style. I can't wait to see what Preston thinks. I can't wait for him to peel me out of it. Now to buy some new underwear to go underneath it. Victoria's Secret, here I come.

The store keeps me busy all day, in fact rushed off my feet is a better description. Paisley and I are closing the store on the twentieth of the month and won't be open again until January the seventh. I can't wait to have a few days off.

We've been advised that the tree lighting ceremony has been moved to this evening due to the mayor having so much on her plate this week.

Dressed in a cute Christmas jumper and jeans, I pull on my Converse and head out of the door. Paisley is dressed similarly but is wearing her favorite knee-length Ugg boots. We link arms as we walk across the square in town to the big Christmas tree.

There's a podium in front of it and plenty of space for people to gather around. It's lovely to see the whole town slowly trickling in. It's always a big thing for the town, coming together for events such as this one. We also have a horse-drawn carriage ready to take people on a ride around the town. The carriage is white, lined with red crushed velvet. The man driving is dressed in black from head to toe, including a top hat. The two gorgeous horses are black and are adorned with red reins. It all looks beautiful and very romantic.

***

"And of course, we wouldn't be standing here today if it wasn't for a certain businessman. He came here to help us get Snowflake back on its feet and, under his guidance, this town has flourished. Ladies and gentlemen, please welcome to the stage, Mr. Preston Fitzgerald."

Applause rings out around me and my cold hands sting from clapping.

Preston takes center stage and clears his throat before speaking.

"Thank you, Mayor Crawford. Ladies and gentlemen, I want to thank you all for welcoming me to your town. I'm the newcomer, but you have all treated me like we've known each other for years. Whether it's Mrs. Vickers in the bakery or Mr. Hogg in the butchers, whether I'm walking around town or having a cup of coffee in the café … I am always treated with kindness. With a smile and a kind word or two. I feel as though this town has well and truly become my home.

I know that when I first arrived in town, people worried that I might ruin it by bringing in big businesses that the small businesses that have been here for generations couldn't compete with. But I never wanted Snowflake to have to compete with anyone or anything. I always wanted it to flourish and grow. I wanted it to be the community it used to be in years gone by.

I'd like to think I'm speaking the truth when I say that my plan seems to have worked. But that is down to all of you, not me. Sure, it was my plan, but it wouldn't have succeeded without the right people making a Herculean effort to come together and make Snowflake what it is today.

So, from the bottom of my heart, thank you all for making me so welcome. But I would be remiss if I didn't thank one person in particular.

Please allow me the indulgence of thanking Miss Aneurin Mackenzie."

I gasp as he says my name. My eyes are glued to him as his seek me out in the crowd.

"Please, Nye, would you join me on stage?"

I feel weird with all the townspeople watching me as I walk to the front of the stage. I don't like all attention being on me.

Preston takes my hand and helps me up the couple of steps onto the wooden stage. He walks back to the podium and keeps hold of my hand. Looking directly at me instead of out into the crowd, he makes me feel like I'm the only person in the world. The noise of the crowd applauding dissipates, and it feels like it's just the two of us.

Looking handsome in his tailored suit, Preston looks at me with a megawatt smile on his face.

"Nye, I think it's true to say that you didn't take a shine to me when I first arrived on the scene in Snowflake. You thought I was a cocky, arrogant, alpha male who wears expensive suits and likes to boss everyone around. And actually, I'd agree with you there, at least in part.

But I would like to think that since you have come to know me, you realize that is not who I am.

When I first got here, you caught my eye. You were beautiful, feisty, a woman who knows her mind and isn't afraid to speak it. None of that has changed, but you have changed me. Your love has changed me. I am not the man I was when I got here. I am so much more. That's because of you. You captivated my heart as well as my soul and I know that loving you is what I was made to do."

I feel tears begin to sting the backs of my eyes and I have to breathe deeply and try my hardest not to let them fall.

Suddenly Preston is no longer standing in front of me…instead, he's down on one knee. A vintage silver ring box is in his open palm. My tears fall unbidden.

"Aneurin Mackenzie, I cannot begin to fathom my life without you in it. I am beginning to think that my life didn't start until I met you. You make me want to be a better man. You make me want things out of life that I never believed possible. I want the dream—the beautiful house, two gorgeous children, the white picket fence, the whole package. But you make me want one thing above all else…"

He swallows, and I see a sudden uncertainty in his eyes. But he isn't uncertain of what he wants, it's my answer he is nervous of.

"Nye, would you do me the greatest honor and agree to be my wife?"

My hands feel sweaty and the neck of my sweater feels like a noose around my neck. I am a nervous wreck. So is Preston, by the looks of it.

"Yes," I whisper, unable to speak any louder.

Taking the ring from the box, Preston takes my left hand and slides it onto my ring finger. I look down at it but cannot see it clearly because of the tears blurring my vision.

Wrapping his arms around me, Preston leans down to claim my lips with his. I pour all my love into kissing him back. All the words I cannot say, all the emotions that are overwhelming me, he absorbs them all.

The loud applause and cheers of the crowd bring me back to reality. Preston releases me and stands next to me with a smile splitting his face. I touch my hand to my face and feel my mirroring smile.

I hold out my left hand in front of me and see it sparkle in the sudden light of the huge tree behind us.

"Congratulations," Mayor Crawford says as she looks at the two of us.

"Congratulations," the crowd echoes around us.

Looking up at Preston, I see my future in an instant. I know in my heart that I was made to love this man. To bear his children. To push him to be the best version of himself as a man, a husband and a father. Just like he will push me to be the best version of myself.

Chapter Nineteen

Preston

I woke up with the biggest smile on my face this morning. I took my time as I slowly made love to my fiancée. I still can't get my head around her saying yes. She took my breath away.

When I went shopping for Christmas decorations for the office party, I was distracted by a jewelry store. I looked in their window and saw the most beautiful platinum ring. After speaking with the jeweler, I learned it was three emerald cut diamonds—one large one in the center, flanked by two slightly smaller ones. The middle stone is just over three carats and the total of the three diamonds takes it to just over five carats. The diamonds are so beautifully clear, absolutely flawless. I could have searched a million jewelry stores and never found another ring to match the beauty of this one. And that's how I feel about my wife-to-be; I could have searched the whole world over and never found another person as amazing as Nye.

God how I hope she never finds out it cost me nearly one hundred grand. She'd castrate me with her bare hands and wear my balls as earrings … or feed them to me.

But I couldn't help it. The moment I saw that ring, I knew it was the one. It could have cost next to nothing, or it could have cost an arm and a leg, I couldn't have cared less. Nye is worth every damn penny.

I got to work before the rest of the staff. I asked Jenny to come in and keep everyone in reception instead of letting them through to their offices. I sent a mass email out last night asking people to come in Christmassy clothing, smart casual would do.

Everything is in full flow—the Christmas music playing in the background, the alcohol is flowing. The only thing missing is my fiancée and her best friend. Trust women to want to make a grand entrance.

The staff were only too happy to be told they'd be partying and then not coming back until the new year. Everyone seems to be in high spirits. I'm actually glad I decided to throw a party. I've never been the stuffy office party type of guy, but this is far from stuffy. There's a relaxed, carefree atmosphere which is just what I hoped for.

My gaze keeps flicking over to the doorway. I'm almost anxious about seeing Nye. Me, anxious. Go figure!

When at last the door opens, it's Paisley I see first. Jack stands from his seat next to me and walks over to greet her.

I wipe my slick palms down my trousers, knowing Nye will be the next person I see. I chose to wear just a shirt and trousers tonight, with my sleeves rolled up and my top button undone. Smart, but casual.

My breath catches in my throat and my heart tries to break free as I see the woman I've been waiting for all night. She looks amazing, sensational, phenomenal.

My trousers begin to feel tight against my budding erection. I have to take some deep breaths before I stand. I don't need my entire staff to see what effect Nye has on me.

Unable to wait any longer to hold her in my arms, I stand and make my way over to Nye. The deep red dress she's wearing is sexy but understated. I love the contrast in materials between the main body of the dress—I'm a man and have no idea what material it is—and the lace of the sleeves and bust and hem detail.

"You look breathtaking, Mrs. Fitzgerald."

"Hey, it's still Mackenzie for now. And who said I was taking your surname? That's rather presumptuous. What if I'm a modern woman who wants to keep her own name?"

I don't answer her, knowing she's doing it just to get a rise out of me. Little does she know she is getting a rise out of me—just not the kind she expected.

I lean down and claim her lips in a soft, sweet kiss. She smells like strawberries and cream. With my hand on her lower back, I guide her to the makeshift dancefloor where we dance to Lady Antebellum's version of "This Christmas".

Dancing with my wife-to-be, laughing with my work colleagues and drinking mulled wine as well as the odd whiskey, I could see this being the first of many office Christmas parties. But the next one will be with Aneurin as my wife.

How I ever got so lucky that this radiant woman agreed to be my eternal soul mate, my forever, I don't know. I must just be the luckiest guy in all of Snowflake, if not the entire universe.

Epilogue

One year later

I'm trembling as I try to tie my knot. Jack swats away my fumbling hands and ties it for me. He grins like the Cheshire Cat as he takes a step back from me and looks me up and down.

"Looking fly, my man."

"Oh please, Jack, never saying 'fly' again, I implore you. You're not one of the cool kids."

We both laugh as he hands me a tumbler of whiskey. Just the one to steel my nerves. I might have to rinse with mouthwash after it though.

I don't know what I have to be nervous about. I'm on the verge of marrying the woman I love with all my heart and soul. Today is the day she finally becomes Mrs. Fitzgerald. A year was too long to wait, but she wanted everything to be perfect. We both did.

Her mother Evelyn and her father Beckett both offered to help pay for the wedding, but I said marrying their daughter was worth every penny. Evelyn ended up paying for the cake and the flowers, whilst Beckett bought her dress. I can't wait to see her walking down that aisle. It doesn't matter what she's wearing, or what flowers she has in her bouquet; all that matters is that she is walking towards the rest of her life with me.

"It's time," Jack says, looking at the watch I bought him for being my best man.

"Then let's go, my friend. Let's go."

We leave the comfort of my house and get into the chauffeur-driven car I hired. My palms are slightly clammy, so I discreetly wipe them on my trousers.

Knowing how much my fiancée likes the "suited and booted" look, I went all out with my suit for today. It's a navy blue, tailored, three-piece suit with an understated checked pattern. I've paired it with a crisp white shirt and a dark red tie.

Once at our destination, we walk inside and see a small number of guests already waiting. They greet us eagerly and I feel my nerves ratchet up. All these eyes on us. What if I fumble my words?

***

The wedding march begins to play, and it takes all I have not to look at her immediately.

Jack gives me a discreet nod when it's time to turn around.

I look to her father, Beckett, first—unable to trust myself to look at my bride without hyperventilating. Who says men don't feel any pressure on their wedding day? We just rock up, say our vows and that's it. We don't feel jittery and on edge. We're men. We're meant to be masculine. Well, who says you're less masculine just because you feel nervous? Not me, that's for sure.

My eyes zone in on my bride and I feel tears begin to sting. She's wearing an off-white gown with spaghetti straps and overlapping pieces of tulle that cascade over each other like a waterfall. The only bling to be seen is the small diamante belt and straps. I can see a hint of her dark red shoes, her nod to it being the festive season.

When we agreed on a Christmas wedding, we didn't want to go overboard with the decorations, so we'd told the wedding planner to keep it minimal but still festive.

As she comes to stand by my side, I look into her eyes and see they are sparkling like the brightest gems, showing she's trying to hold back tears of her own. She looks exquisite. I've never seen anything that could possibly match her beauty. This last year of my life has been the most amazing adventure. With Nye by my side, no two days are ever the same. She moved in with me almost straight away. It took a couple of days to move all of her stuff into the house.

She'd sold her house and put some of the money into her store which is now being run by both her and Paisley. Last year, she gifted Paisley a partnership on Christmas Day. She couldn't have been happier to have her best friend on board.

We'd adopted a gorgeous little pug and named her Ella. But we're not the kind of couple to have their dog as a ring bearer, so she's being looked after by a neighbor today.

I don't remember ever feeling this content in my life. My bride by my side and a whole lifetime to look forward to as man and wife.

***

At the party after the wedding ceremony, the DJ asks us to come to the floor for our first dance as husband and wife. We'd chosen "This Christmas", the song we danced to at the Christmas party last year. It was the first song we danced to as an engaged couple, so it was only fitting to have it as our wedding song too.

As we leave the dance floor, the DJ says it's time for our Secret Santa gift exchange. People have drawn names at random and bought each other gifts. We have all we could ever need, so it was Nye's idea to have our guests buy each other gifts. Unusual? Yes. Typical Nye? Also, yes!

I'm given a long box wrapped in red paper and a silver bow. I wasn't expecting a gift, so I'm wondering what it could be and who it's from.

Everyone is seated to open their gifts and I retrieve a box from inside my jacket pocket. I hand it to Nye and she smiles as she looks down at it.

I look down at the box in my left hand and am momentarily caught by the flash of the ring on my third finger. I can't believe I'm someone's husband. If you'd told me eighteen months ago that I would meet a feisty, stunning, amazing woman and fall so utterly in love with her that I'd propose within mere weeks of being together, I would have said you were bonkers. If you'd told me it would be Nye, I would have said you were even more crazy. That woman couldn't stand the sight of me. Yet here we are. Man and wife. Bound to each other in this life and the next.

Nye clears her throat and it's then I realize I'm still staring at my ring instead of opening my box.

"Merry Christmas, sweetheart," she says in a hushed tone.

"Merry Christmas, Mrs. Fitzgerald."

I lean in and place a kiss on her lips, before withdrawing to open my box.

Looking at the item in the box before me, I am momentarily puzzled. I look at Nye as she smiles a secret smile. Only my wife would be my Secret Santa. And my present? A Christmas miracle. A positive pregnancy test.

Just when I thought my heart couldn't hold any more love, it stretches exponentially to make room for the love I have for our unborn child.

I place my hand on hers and squeeze it gently. My unshed tears can't be held back any longer. Nye places my hand on her stomach, her hand over mine. Just when I thought I was unable to love anyone or anything more, she went and surprised me. I'm going to be a father. Words just cannot do my feelings justice.

As I draw her in for a kiss, Nye whispers in my ear, "Merry Christmas, Daddy."

And just like that, my heart explodes. First husband, now daddy. My life has taken the most unexpected turns to get where I am today and if I could go back and do it all again, I would do it all the same.

As I place the lid back on my box, I see that the little tag reads: *With Love, Your Secret Santa.* The perfect end to a perfect day. But the perfect beginning to a whole new life. A whole new world.

The End

About the author

Keren is a bookworm whose bookshelves groan under the weight of her obsession, but she believes there's always room for "one more book."

She lives in the UK with her son and when she isn't reading or writing, she's nurturing the reader and writer in him as he's currently writing his own book.

Keren loves to connect with her readers. You can reach out to her on social media. She loves to talk anything books, movies and TV.

Her other obsessions include Disney, Marvel, and she's a Potterhead for life.

Also by Keren Hughes

The Jagged Scars Duet

Safe

In every way Elise is a survivor.

As a child, she was abused by the first man she trusted completely.

As a teenager, she was manipulated mentally and physically by a man, to the point that she could not see just how bad their relationship was. She ended up too scared to stay, but even more scared to leave.

Having suffered for years at the hands of men she trusted, she met Jensen. Finally, she felt that she had someone good in her life. Their relationship was all too brief, and when it ended she built a wall around her heart. How could she ever trust a man again?

Elise; a single, disabled mum. It was all too clear that men could not see past her disability. Forsaking the love of men, she concentrated on her son, Caleb. It was the one thing she knew she could do right. Her love for Caleb was beyond measure. He was her whole world. However, Elise's best friend Sam had other ideas, and set her up on a blind date with an extremely hot paramedic.

With so much hurt in the past, she was not sure if she was strong enough to face rejection again. Could she truly open her heart again to another? Could Elise finally find her safe haven in his arms, or would he just add another scar to her soul?

Home

~Home isn't a physical place, it's the place where your heart beats.~

Drew Wright always said he had the "reverse Midas touch"; everything he touched turned to shit instead of gold.

As a child, he was beaten, neglected, and abused by drug-addicted parents whose next fix was more important than having food in the cupboard. Plagued by flashbacks of a past that haunts him, he's worked hard to become a paramedic and help others often caught in the grip of the same trauma he experienced.

After being set up on a blind date with the love of his life he thought he'd lost, it seemed his luck was turning and fate was giving him a second chance. Happily married with two children, he has everything he ever dreamed of.

But then one tragic moment throws his world into upheaval and lands Drew in the middle of a battle to hang on to the life he loves.

Can he separate the past from the present and save his future?

Or will the demons that have stalked him his whole life finally devour him?

Coming soon from Keren Hughes

Out of the Ashes

After the divorce from hell, Jenna Morgan swears off men. But could the town bad boy be the one to make her break that oath?

Freeing herself from the constraints of her ex, she decides to do the one thing she always wanted to but was never allowed: get a tattoo. Nate Peterson is the town bad boy and owner of Blank Canvas tattoo parlour. Walking into his shop could change her life in more ways than one.

Her interfering best friend, Brogan, ropes Jenna into attending a speed-dating event at the local pub where they work. Meeting a guy is the last thing she wants, but Brogan won't let her off the hook that easily.

After meeting business-savvy lawyer, Levi, she's intrigued enough to tick his box on the stupid little card Brogan gave her. But then she bumps into Mr Tall Dark and Brooding and it seems like fate has other plans.

At the insistence of Brogan, she decides to go on a date with each of them. There's no harm in one date, right?! Not realising that something as simple as a date could leave her wanting more, she sees and feels herself falling for the boy from the wrong side of the tracks.

With his brooding exterior and air of mystery, Nate lures her in like a lamb to the slaughter and Jenna finds herself going willingly. But after a couple of crazy months together, a tragedy tears them apart. Nate's grief threatens to drown him, and he finds himself pushing everyone away, including Jenna.

When her controlling mother throws a party that requires her attendance, Jenna finds herself coming face to face with the one she rejected. Feeling conflicted, Jenna walks away before making a choice that threatens to break her heart.

Upon realising his momentous mistake, Nate wants to win her back. But can he earn her trust again?

Will fate help push them back together or will it tear them asunder?

More of our titles

Their Lady Gloriana by Starla Kaye
Cowboys in Charge by Starla Kaye
Her Cowboy's Way by Starla Kaye
Punished by Richard Savage, Nadia Nautalia & Starla Kaye
Accidental Affair by Leslie McKelvey
Right Place, Right Time by Leslie McKelvey
Her Sister's Keeper by Leslie McKelvey
Playing for Keeps by Glenda Horsfall
Playing By His Rules by Glenda Horsfall
The Stir of Echo by Susan Gabriel
Rally Fever by Crea Jones
Behind The Clouds by Jan Selbourne
Trusting Love Again by Starla Kaye
Runaway Heart by Leslie McKelvey
The Otherling by Heather M. Walker
First Submission - Anthology
These Eyes So Green by Deborah Kelsey
Dark Awakening by Karlene Cameron
The Reclaiming of Charlotte Moss by Heather M. Walker
Ryann's Revenge by Rai Karr & Breanna Hayse
The Postman's Daughter by Sally Anne Palmer
Final Kill by Leslie McKelvey

Killer Secrets by Zia Westfield
Crossover, Texas by Freia Hooper-Bradford
The King's Blade by L.J. Dare
Uniform Desire - Anthology
Safe by Keren Hughes
Finishing the Game by M.K. Smith
Out of the Shadows by Gabriella Hewitt
A Woman's Secret by C.L. Koch
Her Lover's Face by Patricia Elliott
Love Times Infinity by K.L. Ramsey
Naval Maneuvers by Dee S. Knight
Love's Patient Journey by K.L. Ramsey
Perilous Love by Jan Selbourne
Patrick by Callie Carmen
Love's Design by K.L. Ramsey
The Brute and I by Suzanne Smith
Love's Promise by K.L. Ramsey
Home by Keren Hughes
Worth the Wait by K.L. Ramsey
The Christmas Wedding by K.L. Ramsey
Only A Good Man Will Do by Dee S. Knight

Our back catalog is being released on Kindle Unlimited
You can find us on
Twitter: BVSBooks
Facebook: Black Velvet Seductions
See our bookshelf on Amazon now!
Search
"BVS Black Velvet Seductions Publishing Company"

11187728R00090

Printed in Great Britain
by Amazon